Izzy held on to Laurie's free hand, then looked at Mark with a slight frown. 'This is the first time you've been here, so you might be a bit scared.'

She gave him a bright smile; she was definitely her mother's daughter, he thought.

'You can hold my other hand, if you like,' she suggested. 'That'll make you feel brave.'

Marc's first instinct was to say no. The idea of holding the little girl's hand, looking as if they were out together on a family outing—when he knew damn well he didn't *deserve* a family—made him feel slightly sick.

But then Izzy smiled at him again, and he felt as if something had cracked inside him. 'Thank you. I'd love to hold your hand.' To his ears, his voice sounded rusty. He glanced at Laurie for direction—was he doing the right thing?—but she was behaving as if absolutely nothing was out of the ordinary.

Together, hand in hand, they walked through coppiced woodlands. Marc could see the odd patch of primroses, and some white flowers he vaguely recognised but didn't have a clue what their names were, but there were no bluebells.

Then Marc caught his breath as they turned a corner and he could see bluebells absolutely everywhere. He'd never seen anything so lovely—and it was so different from London.

'So, are you glad I nagged you into this?' Laurie asked softly.

'Very,' he admitted. 'I wouldn't have missed this for the world.'

'I told you it was special.'

Yes. And so, Marc was beginning to realise, was she.

Dear Reader

This is a story about forgiveness, and how love can give you a second chance.

GP Laurie thinks she's settled and has the perfect life with her daughter and her dog in a little country town—but she's missing something. And Marc needs to forgive himself for the past before he can move on and learn to be happy again.

Working together on a project to help their patients means they're thrown into each other's company—and, although neither intended to fall in love, that's exactly what they end up doing. But it takes a shock for them both to overcome their pasts and admit it...

This book's set in my part of the world, and I can honestly say that the bluebell woods Marc and Laurie visit are even more magical in real life. It's definitely one of the most romantic places in the world, and I'm lucky in that my research assistants are always happy to come with me. (Except the dog, because sadly dogs aren't allowed—otherwise he'd be there, wagging his tail alongside us.)

I'm always delighted to hear from readers, so do come and visit me at www.katehardy.com

With love

Kate Hardy

THE
BROODING DOC'S
REDEMPTION

BY
KATE HARDY

MILLS
BOON®
™

To Maggie Kingsley and Margaret McDonagh—
in loving memory of dear friends who were taken too young.

All the characters in this book have no existence outside the imagination of the author, and have no relation whatsoever to anyone bearing the same name or names. They are not even distantly inspired by any individual known or unknown to the author, and all the incidents are pure invention.

First published in Great Britain 2013
by Mills & Boon, an imprint of Harlequin (UK) Limited.
Large Print edition 2013
Harlequin (UK) Limited, Eton House,
18-24 Paradise Road, Richmond, Surrey TW9 1SR

© Pamela Brooks 2013

ISBN: 978 0 263 23121 2

Harlequin (UK) policy is to use papers that are natural, renewable and recyclable products and made from wood grown in sustainable forests. The logging and manufacturing process conform to the legal environmental regulations of the country of origin.

Printed and bound in Great Britain
by CPI Antony Rowe, Chippenham, Wiltshire

Kate Hardy lives in Norwich, in the east of England, with her husband, two young children, one bouncy spaniel, and too many books to count! When she's not busy writing romance or researching local history she helps out at her children's schools. She also loves cooking—spot the recipes sneaked into her books! (They're also on her website, along with extracts and stories behind the books.) Writing for Mills & Boon® has been a dream come true for Kate—something she wanted to do ever since she was twelve. She's been writing Medical Romances™ for over ten years now. She says it's the best of both worlds, because she gets to learn lots of new things when she's researching the background to a book: add a touch of passion, drama and danger, a new gorgeous hero every time, and it's the perfect job!

Kate's always delighted to hear from readers, so do drop in to her website at www.katehardy.com

Also by Kate Hardy:
in Mills & Boon® Medical Romance™

ONCE A PLAYBOY…
DR CINDERELLA'S MIDNIGHT FLING
ITALIAN DOCTOR, NO STRINGS ATTACHED
ST PIRAN'S: THE FIREMAN AND
    NURSE LOVEDAY *(St Piran's Hospital)*

In Mills & Boon® Modern Romance™

THE HIDDEN HEART OF RICO ROSSI
THE EX WHO HIRED HER
A MOMENT ON THE LIPS

These books are also available in eBook format
from www.millsandboon.co.uk

CHAPTER ONE

THIS was ridiculous. Anyone would think that Marc was five years old and about to start his first day at school, not thirty-five and about to start his first day as a GP at Pond Lane Surgery.

He shook himself. There was absolutely no reason for him to be nervous. If Sam, the senior partner at the practice, hadn't thought that Marc would fit into the team, he wouldn't have offered him the job. Marc had spent ten years working in a busy practice in London. Working in a sleepy country town would be different, but he'd wanted different. Something to help him leave the memories behind.

He took a deep breath and pushed the door open.

The middle-aged woman at the reception desk smiled at him. 'It's a bit early for appointments, I'm afraid. We're not quite open yet.'

'I'm not actually here for an appointment,' he explained. 'My name's Marc Bailey.'

'Oh, our new GP! Welcome to the practice.' She shook his hand. 'I'm Phyllis—well, obviously I'm the receptionist. Sam's expecting you. I'll take you through to his office.'

A friendly face on Reception was a good start. Hopefully the rest of the day would match up to it.

Phyllis rapped on the open door. 'Sam? Marc Bailey's here.' She smiled at Marc. 'I'll leave you to it. If there's anything you need, just let me know.'

'Thank you.'

Sam shook his hand warmly. 'Welcome to Pond Lane. I hope you don't mind, Marc, but I'd like you to work with Dr Grant for the first half of the morning. I know you're perfectly capable of settling in by yourself, but it always helps to have someone teach you the horrible little quirks of a computer system that's new to you.'

'Uh-huh.' Marc wondered where this was leading. Was having someone shadowing him his new boss's way of making sure that he'd made the right decision in offering Marc the job?

'And you'll be helping her at the same time. Laurie works part time at the surgery. She's half-way through qualifying as a GP trainer, and it'll be useful for her to sit in on consultations with someone she hasn't worked with before.'

Marc gave him a wry smile. 'It's been a while since someone observed me in a consultation.'

'Laurie won't bite. She's a sweetie, and she makes the best lemon cake ever,' Sam said with a chuckle.

'Right.' Marc imagined a doctor in her mid-forties, the motherly type, who wanted to enrich her career by teaching new doctors.

'Oh, and I should warn you—she has this pet project. Given your experience in sports medicine, she might ask you to help out.'

Marc wasn't sure whether to be more intrigued or concerned. 'Noted,' he said.

'I'll take you through to Laurie.' Sam shepherded him through to Laurie's room. 'Marc, this is Laurie Grant. Laurie, this is Marc Bailey, our new GP.' He patted Marc's shoulder. 'I'll leave you to sort things out between you.'

'OK.'

Laurie was nothing like Marc had expected.

She was in her early thirties, a couple of years younger than himself, he'd guess, but what he really noticed were the dark corkscrew curls she'd pulled back in a scrunchie, her piercing blue eyes, and the sweetest-looking mouth he'd ever seen.

Which was terrible. He shouldn't even be noticing this sort of thing about her. She was his new colleague, and for all he knew she could be married.

Worse still, he found himself actually glancing at her left hand, to check.

No ring. Not that *that* meant anything.

She didn't seem to notice, and simply held out her hand to shake his. 'Welcome to Pond Lane, Marc.'

When his palm touched hers, it felt like an electric shock.

This really couldn't be happening.

But either it wasn't the same for her, or she was a bit better than he was at ignoring the zing of attraction, because she said, 'It's really good of you to let me sit in on consultations with you this morning, especially as it's your first day here. Leigh, the practice manager, is off today, but she left me all the details so I can set you up on the computer.' She laughed. 'Sam has this mad idea that because I'm the youngest doctor in the practice, it means I'm the one who's best with computers.'

'Are you?' Marc asked.

'Only because my brother's a computer consultant and taught me a lot, to stop me ringing him up and wailing down the phone to him every time I got stuck when I was a student,' she said cheerfully. 'Shall we grab a coffee, then go to your room and make a start?'

'Sure.' Marc found himself warming to her. She was efficient and bubbly, with an overlay of common sense: it was a good combination, and he'd just bet her patients adored her.

They headed for the staff kitchen, and Laurie switched the kettle on. 'Do you prefer tea or coffee?'

'Coffee's great, thanks.' Instant coffee, he noticed. A couple of years ago, he would've been a bit sniffy and insisted on bringing in a cafetière and a special blend of ground beans; and his suit for work would've been a designer label, his shirts hand-made. Nowadays, he knew there were more important things in life. And how he wished he'd been less shallow when he'd been younger. That he'd appreciated what he'd had.

'Milk or sugar?' she asked.

'Just as it is for me, thanks.'

She added a large slug of milk to her own mug, then shepherded him to his consulting room. Which looked incredibly bare: the only hint of colour was the plant on the windowsill. Compared to hers, which had had a child's paintings on the walls and framed photographs on her desk, the room looked impersonal and slightly daunting.

He'd have to change that, to help put his patients at ease. Though, even if all his photos hadn't been packed away, he couldn't quite face putting a photograph on his desk. This was a new start for him. No memories.

There was also a state-of-the-art computer on his desk, he noticed.

'It's probably very similar to the system you used before, but this one does have a couple of quirks.' She switched it on, and fished a note out of the file she carried. 'This is your username and password.'

And he noticed that when she talked him through the system, she let him press the keys rather than rattling through it and expecting him to watch what she did and take it all in. 'You're very good at this teaching stuff.'

'Thank you. It's something I like doing.'

'Is that why you're doing GP training?'

She nodded. 'Sam believes in job enrichment. Ricky—have you met Ricky yet?' At his shake of the head, she said, 'He's not in today, but he has ALS training. We all have our special interests. One of my friends suggested being a GP trainer, because I was always good at explaining things when I was helping others revise for exams. I looked into it and talked to Sam, and an opportunity came up last year to start a course. It means fitting things about a bit—I'm at the university one morning a week in term-time—and my hours are a bit odd, but I'm enjoying it.'

'Sounds good.'

Marc had a lovely voice, and Laurie hoped his manner with patients lived up to it. The last locum at the practice had been terrible, speaking to patients as if they were five years old, and they'd all complained to Phyllis and asked not to have any more appointments with him.

Though Marc was permanent rather than a locum. Given that he was moving here from London, Laurie had expected someone in his late forties or early fifties, wanting to exchange the bustle of life in the city for the much calmer pace of life in a small Norfolk town. Marc looked as if he was in his mid-thirties, a couple of years older than herself. And he was very easy on the eye, with hazel eyes behind wire-framed glasses, and dark hair, cut very short, which stuck up slightly on the top.

She damped down the surge of attraction. This was ridiculous. So what if he happened to remind her slightly of a TV star she'd had a crush on for ages? He probably wasn't single anyway; and, even if he was, she was very careful about relationships nowadays. No way was she giving Izzy a series of 'uncles' flitting in and out of her life in place of her absent father. Her little girl came first. Always would.

Besides, given what had happened with Dean, she didn't want to repeat her mistakes. Being single suited her just fine.

'So who's on your list this morning?' she asked.

He glanced at the screen. 'My first patient's Judy Reynolds.'

'Ah.'

Marc looked at her, frowning. 'Is there anything I need to know?'

'Only that she's on my mental list for my pet project.'

'Sam mentioned that.'

'I thought he might.' She smiled at him. 'I'd better not make you late starting on your first day, but maybe we can talk about my project at break?'

'Sure.'

He pressed the button to call in his first patient, and a few moments later there was a knock at the door.

'Come in,' he called.

A middle-aged woman walked in, and her eyes widened as she saw both Laurie and Marc sitting there.

'Hello, Judy,' Laurie said with a smile. 'I hope you don't mind me sitting in on your appointment with Dr Bailey?'

'Is this all to do with your GP training thing?' Judy asked.

'Yes.' Laurie smiled. 'If anything, Dr Bailey's senior to me—he's been a GP for longer than I have.'

'That's fine. I don't mind you sitting in.'

'Thank you. Just pretend I'm not here,' Laurie said.

Judy looked at Marc. 'So you're not another locum, then?'

'No, I'm here permanently.'

'Right.' She blew out a breath. 'That last locum was terrible—he spoke to you as if you were a toddler.'

Laurie didn't say a word—the practice manager already knew how everyone felt about that particular locum, staff and patients alike—but she wanted to see how Marc dealt with the situation.

'I'm sorry you had that kind of experience with him. But I'd like to assure you that that's not the way I do things, Mrs Reynolds,' Marc said. 'How can I help?'

'I'm probably wasting your time and I'm making a fuss over nothing, but I'm just—' She sighed. 'Well, I'm tired all the time. That locum sent me for blood tests, but I never heard anything back.'

Marc looked at the notes on the screen. 'I can see he checked you out for an underactive thyroid. Can I ask how your periods are?'

'A bit on the heavy side,' she admitted.

'That can make you a bit anaemic, which in turn can make you feel tired,' Marc said.

She grimaced. 'I'm almost looking forward to the menopause so I don't have to put up with them any more.'

'You don't have to put up with heavy periods now, either. It might be another five years before you're menopausal, but periods can often be a problem in the lead-up to menopause. I can give you something to make them a bit more manageable.'

Laurie liked the way he'd got straight to the point without any fuss or embarrassment.

Marc looked at the screen. 'Your blood results tell me your thyroid is working properly, but given that your periods are a bit heavy I'd like to take some blood and check your iron levels, if that's OK?'

Judy nodded.

'In the meantime, you might find it worth taking a supplement with B vitamins and zinc. That often helps with energy levels. Have you been under any extra stress lately?' he asked as he took the blood sample.

Judy shrugged. 'No more than any other mum who's got kids with exams coming up in a few weeks and they have to be nagged into revising.'

'Are you waking up at all in the night?'

'Not that I remember. I sleep like the dead.' She gave him a rueful look. 'Though my husband's been complaining about my snoring, and the kids say we do synchronised snoring.'

He returned her smile. 'And I bet they told you where it'd embarrass you most.'

'In the post office, where everyone could hear them.' She rolled her eyes. 'Yes.'

'It could be that you have sleep apnoea.'

'What's that?' Judy asked.

'It's where the soft tissues in your throat relax when you're asleep and block your airway for a few seconds, which brings your body out of deep sleep. It's so short you won't remember waking up. Even though you might think you've had a good night's sleep, you're not actually getting enough deep sleep to restore your energy levels.'

Laurie liked the way he'd explained it: concisely, and in layman's terms, while putting Judy at her ease. Marc was definitely going to be an asset to the team.

Judy looked worried. 'Do many people get it?'

'It's pretty common. About one in every fifty women of your age get it,' he said. 'But I need to ask you a few more questions to narrow things down a bit more, if you don't mind?'

Marc's manner was as nice as his voice, Laurie was pleased to discover, and he got a lot of information from Judy while keeping his questions relaxed and sounding concerned rather than aggressive.

'Do you have hay fever or anything like that?' he asked finally.

'Well, I often get a bit of a sniffle this time of year.' Judy flapped a dismissive hand. 'But it's nothing I'd bother a doctor with.'

'Any symptom's always worth checking out. That's what I'm here for,' he reassured her. 'I'd like you to have some tests, because from what you've told me I think you might well have sleep apnoea. I'll need to get in touch with the local sleep clinic, but what'll happen is that they'll give you a monitor to wear overnight to measure the oxygen in your blood and your breath, plus your heart rate, and then they'll analyse the data. It'll take me a couple of days to arrange, if that's OK? I'll get Phyllis to ring you as soon as I have some news.'

'Thank you.' Judy looked surprised. 'I'd never even heard of sleep apnoea before.'

'It might not be that,' he reassured her, 'but I think it's a possibility and it's worth checking out. If nothing else, we can cross it off the list of potential causes of your tiredness. You can do some things to help yourself in the meantime. I'm pleased you don't smoke or drink heavily, as that tends to make sleep apnoea worse, but losing weight would help you. So would sleeping on your side rather than your back.'

'How do I do that?' she asked.

'The easiest way is to put a tennis ball in a sock and pin it to the back of your nightie, so it's not comfortable for you to lie on your back.'

'Oh, very sexy,' she said with a grimace. 'My husband's going to wet himself laughing.'

'You said he's snoring, too. If it disturbs you,' Marc said, 'then you can do the same thing to his pyjamas. And tell him it's on your doctor's advice.' Mark smiled.

'I'll do that.' She smiled.

'Now—your periods. It says here you're not on the Pill.'

'No. John had the snip after our son was born.'

'OK. Have you had any problem with taking any tablets with progesterone in the past?'

'No.'

'Good. It's oestrogen that's making your periods heavy, and the progesterone will help balance that out a bit. You take the tablets for twenty-one days and then stop for seven, and you should find that your periods are a lot more manageable.'

'Thank you.'

'Losing weight,' he said gently, 'would help you with that as well. Your body produces more oestrogen when you're overweight.'

Judy looked upset. 'It's not as if I sit there watching TV all night, stuffing my face with doughnuts and burgers.'

'No,' he replied carefully, 'but your body's less

efficient as you get older, so every year after you hit forty you'll need to exercise more and eat less to stay at the same weight. Which is totally unfair, but I guess at least it happens to all of us.'

'Can I suggest something?' Laurie asked. At Marc's nod, she continued, 'I'm about to set up a project for some of our patients who are having problems losing weight. It's not a judgemental thing, it's looking at ways we can support you better and help you. Would you like to come along and see what's on offer?'

'After all the diets I've been on, it's worth a try,' Judy said. 'All right.'

'Great. I'll put you down on my list, and I'll get in touch with more details later in the week,' Laurie said.

Marc printed out the prescription, signed it and handed it to Judy. 'I'll get Phyllis to ring you and make an appointment as soon as I hear back from the sleep clinic.'

'Thank you, Dr Bailey.'

'Pleasure. And I meant what I said. If you're worried about something, no matter how silly you think it is, come and see me. If it's something you don't need to worry about, I can tell you so you can stop worrying—and if it *is* something to worry about, then by telling me we've got a better chance of catching it early, which in turn means that treatment will be easier for you.'

'I will.' She looked relieved. 'Thank you, Dr Bailey.'

'My pleasure.'

Marc saw the rest of his patients up to the mid-morning break, then glanced at Laurie. 'Dare I ask if I passed muster?'

She rolled her eyes. 'It wasn't a test. It was a chance for me to observe how you do things, and maybe learn from you. But, since you asked, yes, you have the skills I'd want my trainees to have. You put patients at their ease, you talk to them in layman's terms, and you're a definite improvement on that locum.'

'Thank you. Though, from what I've heard this morning, just about *anyone* would be an improvement on that locum.' He raised an eyebrow. 'So how did Mrs Reynolds know about your training?'

'This is a small town, Marc. Everyone knows everything.'

'Right.'

He sounded slightly tense—wary about living his life in a goldfish bowl, maybe. She smiled. 'It's not being nosey, it's *caring*. It's being part of the community. Talking of which, my pet project might be useful for you. Obviously you don't need to lose weight, but it'll be a quick way for you to get to know a lot of people in the town.'

'So what does it involve?'

'Let's grab a drink, and I'll explain.' In the staff kitchen, she made them both a coffee, then chose a corner chair. 'We have quite a few patients on the obesity register. I'm looking at trying to stop them developing diabetes or having a CV incident. It's not all about diet—a few of them have brought in food diaries, and they've already made all the simple switches and are eating sensibly.'

'What about exercise?' Marc asked.

'That's what I think the problem is. They already have work and family commitments, and they put their own needs way down the list and they don't think they have the time to exercise.'

'So we have to change their mind sets first.'

'Exactly. A friend of mine at the university is doing a study on the effects of diet and exercise in people over thirty-five. He can lend us activity monitors, so we can get our at-risk patients to wear them for a week and we can show them a baseline of what they actually do, and then we look at how they can boost their activity, when and where.'

'Sounds good.'

'I thought we could repeat the monitoring at three-month intervals to see how the activity patterns of our patients have changed, and tie that in with weight, blood glucose and cholesterol checks. It's a win-win situation. My friend Jay gets people in his target group for his study, and we get to help our patients. And the monitors won't cost anything, so Leigh won't be on my case about budgets.'

'Ah, the joys of budgets. The key to getting people to do regular exercise is to find out what they actually enjoy doing,' Marc said.

She was pleased that he'd hit the nail on the head. 'That's why I want to get the local gyms and sports clubs involved, to set up taster sessions and beginners' classes. Once our patients find out what they enjoy doing, then we talk them into having an exercise buddy who goes with them to whatever the activity is.'

'So they feel they can't let their friends down and they stick to a programme,' Marc said. 'That's a really good idea.'

'Sam says you have an interest in sports medicine.'

'Yes.' Though Marc didn't volunteer any information about himself or what experience he had in sports medicine, Laurie noticed. Clearly he preferred to keep himself to himself. OK. She could work with that. She'd seen how he was with patients, and that was more important.

'So would you like to be involved in the project?' she asked.

'I can't really say no, can I?'

'Of course you can. I understand if you're too busy.'

He looked thoughtful, and for a moment she thought he was going to say no. Then he nodded. 'OK.'

'Thank you. When's a good time for you for a meeting?'

'After surgery?' he suggested.

Not when she had a pile of paperwork and then

had to take the dog out and do the school run. 'Is there any chance you could make an evening meeting at my house?' she asked hopefully.

'Your house,' he repeated.

'Because I'm a single mum,' she explained. 'It'd be a lot easier for me to discuss work with you at my place after Izzy's gone to bed. If that's a problem for you, never mind—I'll ask my mum to babysit.'

Something in her tone told Marc that wasn't her preferred option. 'But you'd rather not?'

'Mum helps me out quite a bit as it is,' Laurie admitted. 'I try not to ask her unless it's really desperate, because it's not fair to keep relying on her.'

Discuss the project at her house.

A family home.

It was something Marc had shied away from for the last couple of years; since the accident, he'd quietly cut himself off from friends who had children. But right now it didn't look as if he had much choice in the matter. Given that Laurie had already explained why she didn't want to ask her mum, he'd feel mean if he pushed her into getting a babysitter. And he didn't want to explain why children were difficult for him, outside work. That was his business. His burden.

'If it's a problem for your partner,' she added, misreading his silence, 'then she—or he—is very welcome to join us. We won't be discussing individual patients, so we wouldn't be breaking any confidentiality.'

His partner was welcome to join them.

Marc just about managed not to flinch.

'I don't have a partner,' he said, struggling to keep his voice even. It was something he'd just about come to terms with over the last two years. But he still couldn't forgive himself for Ginny's death.

Laurie grimaced. 'Sorry. You must think I'm being horribly nosey. I guess that's the problem with growing up in a small town—you know everyone and everyone knows you, and if you don't know something you tend to come straight out and ask. It wasn't meant maliciously.'

He understood that—he'd already worked out that Laurie Grant was warm, bubbly and incredibly enthusiastic—but he didn't want people knowing too much about him. If they knew the truth about his past, they'd despise him as much as he despised himself. 'Uh-huh,' he said neutrally.

'How about this evening?' she suggested.

'That's fine. What time's good for you?'

'Izzy goes to bed at seven. So any time after that.' She shrugged. 'Unless you'd like to come for dinner? It's nothing fancy, just pasta and garlic bread and salad, but there's more than enough if you'd like to join us.'

'Thanks, but I'll take a rain check if you don't mind.' He didn't want to be rude to his new colleague; but he was also guiltily aware that in other circumstances he would've loved to share a meal with her. There was something about Laurie that drew him; she wasn't a conventional beauty, but there was a warmth and brightness about her, and her smile made the room feel as if it had just lit up. Though, for his own peace of mind, he knew he needed to keep himself separate. And in any case he'd guess that, as a single parent, her life would be complicated enough without adding someone like him to the mix.

'No problem.' She scribbled down her address on a piece of paper, added her phone number and handed it to him. 'Just in case you get held up. See you later.' She smiled. 'Enjoy your first morning, and welcome to Pond Lane Surgery.'

The rest of the morning surgery went fine. Marc went home for a sandwich and ate it in the kitchen. He stayed out of the dining room, because it contained a stack of boxes he hadn't been able to face unpacking. Boxes full of memories he couldn't handle.

Maybe he should've taken up his sister's offer of help, instead of being too proud and telling Yvonne that he was fine and he'd be able to sort it out. Because he wasn't fine. And he couldn't sort it out.

Still, he'd brushed her offer aside, so he'd have to live with his choice. The boxes couldn't stay there for ever, so he'd have to make himself do it room by room.

One step at a time.

CHAPTER TWO

MARC wasn't in the mood for cooking when he got home from an afternoon of house calls. He made himself a salad and ate it listlessly—food nowadays was fuel, rather than a pleasure—then looked up Laurie's address on his satnav. Her house was totally the other side of the town from his, far enough to justify using the car rather than walking.

When he parked his car outside and walked up the path to her front door, he wished he'd thought to bring her some flowers or something. OK, so this was a work meeting rather than a social event, but it was still being held at her house, and he felt uncomfortable turning up without anything. Then again, would flowers be making the wrong kind of statement?

He shook himself. Oh, for pity's sake. He needed to be professional about this. But he was horribly aware that this whole situation was throwing him. He was about to walk into just the kind of home he could've had if the accident hadn't happened. A family home. One with children.

But the accident *had* happened. He had a bachelor pad, not a family home. And he only had himself to blame.

He knocked on the front door. There a brief woof and a 'Shh!', and then Laurie opened the door. A chocolate Labrador with a wagging blur of a tail was desperately trying to barge past her. There was a smudge of flour on Laurie's face and several of her dark corkscrew curls had escaped from the scrunchie she used to hold her hair back. The whole effect was unbelievably cute, and he found himself wanting to tuck the stray curls into place and brush that smudge of flour from her skin.

Which was incredibly dangerous. He didn't need that kind of contact. Didn't want it. His heart had been broken, he was still trying to patch it up, and no way was he ever risking any kind of relationship again, other than on a strictly colleagues basis. He even kept his family at a distance nowadays, because it was easier. If he didn't let himself feel, he wouldn't hurt.

Misinterpreting his sudden stillness, she pushed the dog back behind her. 'Sorry, Cocoa's a bit over-friendly.' Within a nanosecond, the dog was trying to push past her again. 'I forgot to ask if you're OK with dogs. I can put him in the utility room, if you'd rather.'

'No, it's fine. I like dogs.' It had even been part of his and Ginny's plans. A baby, and then a dog. A house with a garden.

Ginny would've loved the old cottage he'd found to rent in the small Norfolk town. She would've loved the duck pond on the green, the ancient flint church with its round tower, the gentle undulations of the countryside around them. But because of his own stupidity he had nobody to share it with. Nobody to love. Nobody to love him back.

He pushed the thoughts away and held out his hand for the dog to sniff, then scratched the top of the dog's head. There was a look of sheer bliss on Cocoa's face and he leaned towards Marc.

'He'll be demanding a fuss from you all night,' Laurie warned with a smile. 'Come in. I hope you don't mind, but I'm waiting for some stuff to come out of the oven, so we need to stay in the kitchen. Can I get you a coffee, or maybe a glass of wine?'

Definitely not wine. That had been one of the causes of his downfall, and he hadn't touched a drop since the funeral. 'Coffee would be lovely, thanks,' he said politely.

'Come in and sit down.'

It was clearly a family kitchen. There were several paintings held on the fridge with magnets, obviously the work of a young child. And if that wasn't enough proof, there was a cork board on one wall covered with school notices and photographs of a little girl, varying from babyhood to what looked like about five years old.

Marc couldn't help thinking how his own child would've been eighteen months old now, toddling everywhere and starting to chatter away. A boy or a girl? It had been too soon to tell.

He dug his fingernails into his palms, and the slight pain was just enough to stop him thinking and ripping the scars off his heart.

On the worktop, there was a plate full of cupcakes covered in very pink icing, along with lots of sparkly sprinkles—and there were almost as many on the worktop as there were on the cakes. A pile of washing-up was stacked up next to the sink and a batch of cookies sat on a cooling wire rack next to the oven. Clearly Laurie was in the middle of a baking session.

She followed his gaze when she turned round from the kettle and winced. 'Sorry, it's a bit untidy. I meant to clear up properly before you got here, but then Izzy wanted me to read her bedtime story a second time, and—' She spread her hands. 'Well, you know how it is with kids.'

Not personally. And he never would now. He didn't deserve to have a family. 'Yes,' he said, as neutrally as he could.

Cocoa sat at Marc's feet and rested his chin on Marc's knee; absently, Marc rubbed the top of the dog's head.

'Would you like a cookie with your coffee?' Laurie asked.

'Thank you. But I hope you didn't go to all this trouble for me.'

'No, of course n—' She winced, cutting the word off as she put a couple of cookies onto a plate. 'Sorry, that came out the wrong way. I didn't mean you weren't worth taking any trouble over. I'm baking because it's the PTA coffee morning tomorrow. Izzy decorated the cakes.'

Laurie's little girl. Which explained the sprinkles, and probably most of the mess.

'Obviously I don't get a chance to actually go to the coffee morning because I need to be at the surgery for my shift, but I try to do my bit to help. I always make them some cakes to sell, give them a raffle prize and leave them money for some tickets. If they draw my name out, they choose something for me and send the prize home with Izzy.'

Laurie was clearly very involved with village life. Not only was she a GP, she was also a mum who did things to support the local school. Would Ginny have been like that? he wondered. Probably. As a teacher, she would've been involved with the school, either because she worked there or because their child went there. Though she would've been a bit less chaotic than Laurie. Their house in London had never been as untidy as this.

'So did you enjoy your first day at the practice?' she asked.

Work. He could talk about work, he thought gratefully. Not personal stuff. That was good. 'Fine.'

'Good.' Laurie put a mug of coffee in front of him, along with the cookies, then added milk to her own coffee and sat down opposite him. 'I've been thinking about the easiest way to tackle this. I thought we could maybe brainstorm all the different kinds of exercise we can think of, then I'll list all the people within a five-mile radius who can offer each one, and we can divvy up the calls between us and ask them if they'd be prepared to do a taster session for us.'

'Sure. That sounds reasonable.'

She looked relieved. 'Great. One tiny thing: would you mind if I asked you to deal with Neil Peascod? He owns the gym and swim place at the other end of the town.'

'Do I take it he's likely to be difficult?' Marc asked, wondering why she didn't want to deal with the guy.

'Not exactly.' She flushed. 'He was a bit, um, persistent with me last year. I guess he didn't like to think that someone might actually say no to him.'

'He asked you out?' Then Marc realised how rude that sounded. 'I apologise. I didn't meant it to come out like that.'

Laurie didn't look in the slightest bit offended. She simply laughed. 'Don't worry, I'm under no illusions that I'm the next supermodel. I'm thirty years old, I'm a mum, I have lumpy bits, and I have days when my hair needs stuffing under a hat so nobody can see how frizzy it looks.' She smiled. 'And I also have days when I look utterly fabulous. But they're the rare ones. Dog-walking isn't exactly the time or place to wear a little black dress and high heels.'

At the W-word, the Labrador deserted his post at Marc's feet, rushed over to Laurie, put his paws on her knee and licked her face hopefully. She rolled her eyes and petted him. 'No, Cocoa, I didn't mean *now*. You know as well as I do that walkies is when I get home from work and before I collect Izzy from school.'

Marc couldn't help smiling. He liked Laurie. She was warm and bubbly, yet at the same time she was very down-to-earth.

'Sorry about that.' When she switched her attention back to him, he noticed just how blue her

eyes were. Almost as bright as the forget-me-
nots in his garden. 'Neil. No, he's not *difficult*.
He just thinks that he's the answer to a desperate
single mum's problems.' She wrinkled her nose.
'Yes, I'm a single mum but, no, I'm not desperate, I don't necessarily need a man in my life to
make it complete, and I'm doing just fine, thank
you very much.'

She didn't sound bitter, but as if she was simply stating the facts. Or was that a gentle warning to him? Marc wondered. He'd told her that
he was single. Perhaps this was her way of telling him that even if he might be interested, she
wasn't.

'Noted,' he said drily. He took a bite of the
still-warm cookie. 'This is very nice.'

'Thank you. And please don't let Cocoa con
you into sharing with him. They're bad for his
teeth, and he's very far from being a poor, starv-
ing hound.'

The dog looked up at him with mournful eyes,
and Marc couldn't help smiling. 'Not according
to him.'

'He's an old fraud.' She smiled back. 'Sam said

you were interested in sports medicine. Is that what you did in your last job?'

'It was more of a spare-time thing, really. I worked with the local rugby club.'

'Oh. Do you play?' she asked.

'Not any more.' Marc found himself volunteering information; he hadn't expected that and it unnerved him slightly. 'I was injured.'

'Knee?' she guessed.

'Shoulder. Dislocation, then a rotator cuff tear.'

'Ouch.' She looked sympathetic. 'I'm not surprised you stopped playing. In your shoes, I wouldn't want to risk doing that again.'

'Believe me, after three months of doing nothing but triage calls because my arm was out of action, I'd never risk it again.' And he wished with all his heart that he hadn't given in to the frustration he'd felt at having to give up the game he loved. Because then maybe he could've stopped the chain of events that had wrecked his life and robbed him of everything else he loved.

'I guess rugby and football probably wouldn't be the best kind of exercise for our group anyway,' she said.

'I'd say no to squash as well,' he said.

'Very sensible. And we'll ban them from jogging. We're trying to improve their circulation, not give them shin splints.'

'Or overdoing it in the first flush of enthusiasm and giving themselves a heart attack.' He looked thoughtfully at her. 'Badminton's a possible.'

'And swimming. As well as low-impact exercise classes and circuit training,' she suggested.

'Maybe martial arts—kick-boxing doesn't have to be fast and furious.'

She smiled. 'I've always fancied trying that one myself.' She took a laptop from a drawer in the huge pine dresser. 'Let's start getting this down.' The computer whirred and made a couple of protesting noises, and she rolled her eyes. 'Sorry, this is a bit old. I'm afraid it takes ages to boot up.'

His own was state of the art and would've been ready to go by now. As a single mum, Laurie would have to juggle her finances, and a new computer probably wasn't top of her priorities, Marc thought.

They made a list together. Halfway through it, the timer on the oven beeped.

'Sorry, do you mind if I sort this out?' she

asked. 'The topping works best if you do it when the cake's hot.'

'I take it that's for school?' He grinned.

'Yes.' She smiled. 'But, if you're good, I'll make a cake for the surgery later in the week.'

It smelled wonderful, and Marc ignored the fact that this was the first time he'd been interested in food in a very, very long time. 'I'm good,' he said. 'If you can talk at the same time as you do whatever it is you're doing to the cake, I'll take over the typing.'

'Excellent. Thanks.'

Marc surreptitiously watched her as she took the cake out of the oven, pierced the top with a skewer and spooned the contents of a bowl over it. She looked up and caught him looking at her. 'It's lemon and sugar.'

The citrus scent made his mouth water. 'Is this the one Sam told me about?'

'Yes. It's his favourite. So, are you going to do some typing or just hoping for cake, like Cocoa is?'

He couldn't help smiling. 'I'm typing. Start talking.'

Within twenty minutes they had a good list.

They worked through it again and weeded out some of the more unlikely suggestions they'd come up with.

'This looks good to me. I'll work my way through it and put in the contacts, and then give you your half of the list tomorrow,' Laurie said.

'That's fine,' Marc said. 'And I guess I'd better let you get on.' Especially as he felt way too comfortable here. And that unnerved him.

She smiled at him. 'Thanks. Sadly, the washing-up won't do itself, and it'd be a bit self-indulgent to have a dishwasher when there's only Izzy and me living here. Are you sure you don't want another coffee before you go?'

'I'm sure, but thanks for the offer. See you to-morrow.'

There was something lost about the expression in Marc's eyes, Laurie thought when Marc had gone. Had he been through a bad divorce? That might explain why he'd come here from London. Maybe she could find a tactful way of talking to him and help him understand that it did get better eventually.

OK, so she hadn't actually been married to

Dean, but the break-up and then sorting out everything afterwards had been tough. The only thing missing had been the fight in court; the rest of the acrimony and guilt had been there.

Just as Marc had left, she'd wanted to put her arms round him, hold him close and tell him not to worry because everything was going to work out just fine. Which was crazy. She barely knew the man. And she certainly wasn't looking for any complications in her own life.

Then again, she'd been lucky. She'd had people there for her when her own life had hit the skids. And she had the strongest feeling that Marc didn't. He was a stranger to the area. He could do with a friend. OK, so when she'd come home she'd been far from a stranger—but she knew what that felt like, to need a friend. So it would be mean of her to back off and ignore him… Wouldn't it?

CHAPTER THREE

ON WEDNESDAY morning, Marc walked into his surgery to find a plate on his desk containing a cupcake exactly like the ones he'd seen in Laurie's kitchen the previous night, along with a printed copy of the table he and Laurie had made together, detailing the different exercise providers and which of them was going to call each one, with space to scribble notes.

That cake gave him an odd feeling. Was this the sort of thing his own child would've done with Ginny, making cakes and decorating them haphazardly and sending him off to work with one? A little thing, made with such love...

He shook himself as he heard a rap on the door, a nanosecond before it opened. Sam, the senior partner, leaned round the door. 'Morning, Marc. How are you settling in?'

'Fine, thanks.' Marc summoned up a professional smile, not wanting Sam to see how much the cupcake had thrown him.

'I meant to say yesterday, Ruth said you're very welcome to come to ours for lunch on Sunday. It's not much fun having weekends on your own and it takes a while to settle into a small country town, especially when you're used to the city.'

Marc appreciated the overture of friendship but he'd learned that, once people knew about his past, any friendship tended to come tempered with pity. He had quite enough pity for himself without needing it from others. 'Thanks. That's really kind of you, but I have a few things to sort out.'

'Sure. Well, you know where we are if you change your mind. Just turn up.'

'Thanks. I will.' Though Marc had no intention of doing so. He didn't deserve such kindness. Not after the way he'd messed up.

Sam glanced at the cupcake and smiled. 'Oh, good. I hoped we'd get some of the leftovers from the PTA baking session. Laurie's cakes are wonderful.' He laughed. 'Even if Izzy does put half a ton of sprinkles on every single one.'

Marc carefully sidestepped the subject of children. 'Laurie and I brainstormed the project last night.' He waved the table at Sam. 'She's added the contact details, and we're splitting the calls between us.'

'Excellent.' Sam looked pleased. 'I can see you're going to fit right in. We definitely made the right choice, asking you to join us.'

'Thank you. I hope I live up to that.'

Marc didn't get the chance to see Laurie during surgery as she was busy on house calls and, because she worked part time, she finished earlier than he did. After he'd seen his last patient for the day, he looked at his watch. Laurie's place was on his way home from the surgery. He knew he probably ought to call her first and make arrangements to discuss the project, but he couldn't resist the impulse to drop in and see her.

And he didn't want to analyse the reason too closely.

'Oh, Marc.' She looked flustered when she opened the front door.

'Sorry, is this a bad time?'

'No, but my house is chaos city at this time of day, so I'll have to ask you to ignore the mess.

Izzy's drawing pictures at the kitchen table. Come in, and I'll put the kettle on.' Her smile brightened back into a welcome.

And that was half the reason he was here.

Because that smile drew him. Made him feel that the world was a better place.

Marc followed Laurie into the kitchen, where a little girl was sitting at the kitchen table. Cocoa was sitting patiently by the child's feet, clearly hoping for a share in the cake that sat on the plate beside her. He wagged his tail at Marc, but didn't leave his position or break his eyeline from the table.

'Izzy, this is Dr Bailey. He's come to work with me at the surgery and he's just popped in to see me about a project we're working on together.'

The little girl looked up at him. 'Hello, Dr Bailey,' she said shyly.

'Marc, this is Izzy, my daughter.'

'Hello, Izzy.' He looked at Laurie. 'She's very like you.' She had the same wild dark curls, though they weren't tied back neatly like Laurie's hair was; and Izzy's eyes were a deep brown rather than a piercing blue.

'I've got a new friend at school,' Izzy said.

'Her name's Molly. She moved here last week and she only started in our class yesterday. I said she could play with me and Georgia at playtime so she won't be lonely.'

Taking the new girl under her wing—just as Laurie was taking him under her wing, Marc thought. Like mother, like daughter. 'That's very kind of you,' he said.

'Me and Mummy made some cakes. Would you like one?' Izzy asked.

'No, thank you.'

She nodded sagely. 'Because you don't want to spoil your dinner.'

Marc was torn between wanting to smile—he'd just bet that particular phrase came from Laurie—and panicking. He wasn't used to this. He'd kept himself separate for so long; contact with a child, outside work, spooked him slightly.

'That's right,' he said. 'But your mum brought some of your cakes into work this morning and I had one then. It was very nice.'

She beamed at him. 'Did you like the sprinkles?'

No. He'd scraped them off, along with most of the icing; it had been a little too sweet for his taste. 'They were delicious,' he said, not wanting to spoil it for her.

'I like sprinkles.'

He couldn't help smiling. He'd already worked that one out for himself.

'Would you like a glass of milk?'

She really was her mother's daughter—warm, sweet and generous. And it scared the hell out of him.

'Thank you for the offer but I'm fine, thanks.'

'Grown-ups normally have coffee or tea, Iz,' Laurie said, putting her arms round her daughter's shoulders and resting her face against her little girl's.

It was just how Marc had imagined Ginny would be with their child, and it sent a shockwave through him. He really, really wished he hadn't given in to that impulse to call in and see her. If only he'd waited until this evening, or had called her first to arrange a time when Izzy would be in bed…

'But I'm not allowed to use the kettle. I'm too little,' Izzy pointed out.

'I know, sweetheart.' Laurie kissed her. 'Do you want to do another drawing for me? I need to talk to Dr Bailey about work. We won't be long, I promise.'

He was eating into Laurie's family time, and that wasn't fair. And seeing Izzy, the love between parent and child—something he'd wanted so badly and would never have now—made him want to back away. Fast.

'Did you want a coffee, Marc?' Laurie asked.

'No, thanks, I'm fine. I only called in because I was passing and I thought it'd be just as quick to drop in as it would be to ring you later.'

He looked nervous, and Laurie didn't have a clue why. 'Good idea,' she said.

'I wanted to let you know that I've had a good response already from the calls I've made. But do you have a slot booked on a regular basis in a hall or something, or will our patients need to go to a different place each week?'

'I thought we'd try and keep everything in the same place, because then there's less chance of any confusion and also no excuses for not turning up,' Laurie said. 'I'm waiting for a phone call to confirm it, but I'm pretty sure we've got the village hall on Wednesdays at eight. Sam says we can use the surgery's waiting room for the talks from the cardiologist, diabetic specialist and nutritionist, if we need to, but obviously it's not a suitable space for an exercise class. Even a small one.'

'Great. I'll call my contacts back to pencil in some dates, then. Oh, and I hope I haven't stomped all over your toes, but I drafted a letter to the patient group over lunchtime. Do you want me to email it to you, so you can see if I've missed anything or there's something you think needs changing?'

'That'd be great, thanks. It's probably easier to send it here than to the surgery. Do you have my email address?'

'No.'

She scribbled it down on a piece of paper and handed it to him. For a second, their fingers touched, and awareness surged through her; she damped it down swiftly. This wasn't appropriate. Wrong time, wrong place. And probably wrong man; she didn't exactly have a good track record in that department.

'Thanks. I'll, um, see you tomorrow. And I'll email you that letter when I get home.'

'OK.'

'Bye, Izzy.' Though he didn't go over to the little girl or so much as look at her drawing, let alone comment on it.

Not that Izzy seemed upset by it. She was too busy colouring in her picture. 'Bye bye, Dr Bailey.' She smiled at him, and Laurie's heart clenched with love for her daughter.

Was it her imagination, or had Marc gone very, very still?

Imagination, she decided, and saw him out.

But over the rest of the evening, she wondered. Did Marc have children and his divorce had been so acrimonious that he didn't have access to them? Then again, she had a fairly good instinct about people, and she didn't think Marc was the unreasonable type that would make any solicitor wary of allowing him access. Maybe it was something else, she thought. Something sadder, because Marc had definite shadows in his eyes.

Just before afternoon surgery the next day, there was a rap on Marc's consulting-room door. Expecting it to be Sam, he looked up with a smile, and felt his eyes widen as he saw Laurie.

Which was ridiculous. She was his colleague; she'd made it clear that she was perfectly fine being single; and, even if she had been in the market for a relationship, Marc knew he was too damaged to be able to offer her anything.

'Hi. You OK?' she asked.

'Sure.'

She waited, and he sighed. 'No.'

'Tough morning?'

He nodded. 'Something like that.'

She came into the room and sat on the chair his patients used. 'Want to talk about it?'

'I can't dump it on you. Anyway, it's nearly time for us to see our next patients.'

'True.' She looked at him. 'If you're not busy tonight, you could come over and tell me then.'

'Dr Fixit?' he asked.

'That's what I do,' she said lightly. 'What you do, too.'

'Not in this case.'

She reached over to squeeze his hand, and the contact made his skin tingle. 'Marc, we all get patients where we can't make everything all right for them. Nobody else would be able to fix it either, so don't blame yourself.'

Easier said than done. He blamed himself for a lot of things.

And then she gave him that light-up-the-room smile. 'I could give you my trainee pep talk. Which would be immensely cheeky of me, given that you're more experienced than I am.'

'It would,' he agreed. But that smile had done a lot to ease his soul.

'Up to you. I'm not busy tonight—well, once I've read Izzy a bedtime story or six. So if you want to talk about it, come over.'

'Why are you asking me?' He grimaced. 'Sorry. That was ungracious.'

'But a fair comment. I'm asking you because I do the same job as you. Unless you have family or friends who do, too, they won't really get what you're feeling right now and why. Plus you're new around here, and could maybe do with a local friend.'

Friendship. That was what she was offering. 'Thank you.' He felt incredibly humbled.

She smiled at him. 'I actually came to say that

letter you wrote was perfect. I'll do a mail merge and send them all off today,' she said.

'Great.' And how ridiculous that her approval pleased him so much. She was his colleague. He knew he was good at his job. He didn't need approval from her. But it still warmed him. 'Your daughter's very like you.'

And why on earth had he said that?

'The spit of me at that age, but with brown eyes,' Laurie agreed with a smile.

'I didn't mean just in looks. It's the way she is. Warm and open.'

Oh, now, he *really* hadn't meant to come out with that. He didn't want her thinking that he was pursuing her, the way the gym guy had last year. Because he wasn't pursuing her. Was he?

Her smile widened. 'Thanks. I'm trying to give her the best view of life and other people—and I don't want her to think it matters that she doesn't have a dad.'

'Of course it doesn't.'

Though Marc couldn't help wondering what had gone wrong with the marriage. He couldn't imagine anyone being daft enough to let Laurie go.

And that was an even more dangerous thought. Laurie Grant was sweet and warm and chaotic, and she most definitely didn't need any more complications in her life. Especially a complication like him. 'My patient's here,' he said, gesturing to the screen on his desk. 'Better not keep him waiting.'

'No.' She got up and walked to the door. 'See you later, maybe.'

Marc couldn't stop thinking about Laurie all afternoon. And he found himself going over to her place later that evening. Izzy was in bed, to his relief, and Laurie had tidied up. He wondered if she'd done it specially.

'Yes,' she said, 'I did tidy up in case you came over.'

He groaned. 'I'm sorry. Did I say that aloud?'

'No, but it was written all over your face.'

He felt the colour seep into his cheeks. 'I'm sorry. I wasn't criticising you.'

'I know, but it was chaos city here and it'd gone beyond even *my* mess tolerance levels.'

She made coffee, and ushered them through to her living room. There were pictures everywhere, more even than he could remember Ginny having in their house. 'So tell me about your patient.'

'She's about our age, and had cysts on both ovaries. The surgeon couldn't save them. And now she wants a baby and can't have one without help.' He sighed. 'I really feel for her.' Especially as it had ripped the top off his own scars. Elaine Kirby had said how much she wished she'd starting thinking about a baby earlier, instead of leaving it until her career was settled and she'd saved up enough to extend her maternity leave. And how Marc wished he and Ginny hadn't waited so long either...

'IVF?'

'Her husband isn't keen—it's not the money, it's the emotional upheaval and what she'd have to go through physically. And she's not sure about adoption—even though it's the being there that makes you a parent, not the biology.'

'That's very true.'

He grimaced. 'Sorry. That wasn't meant to be a pop at you.'

'I know.' She brushed it aside. 'Poor woman.

That's a tough situation. But you can't fix everything, Marc.'

'You try,' he pointed out.

'Yes, and I always will. But you have to be realistic. Some things you can't fix.'

'I'm sending her for counselling.'

'Which is exactly what I would've done, too.'

'It doesn't feel like enough.'

He sounded so miserable. And Laurie wanted to cheer him up. 'Maybe not now, but these things take time.' She looked at him. 'I have an idea. Something that will make you feel better.'

'Dr Fixit again?'

'Absolutely.' And the fact that Marc Bailey was utterly gorgeous…well, that had nothing to do with this. A relationship wouldn't be a good idea for either of them. But friends she could do. 'Are you busy on Sunday?'

'Why?' he asked, sounding wary.

'Because,' she said, 'you're new to the area and there's something special you probably don't know about but you need to see, and it really has to be *this* weekend.'

His eyes narrowed. 'What does?'

'Something,' she said softly, 'that I always came home for at this time of year. Even when we were really busy at the practice in London.'

He blinked. 'You lived in London?' He sounded surprised, as if he hadn't expected that.

'I haven't always worked in a small town.' She smiled to take the sting from her words. 'I trained in London, and I worked as a GP there after I qualified. I decided to come back home when Izzy was born. It was probably a bit selfish of me, but I needed my family's support, and I'm glad I made that decision. So, shall I pick you up at nine on Sunday?'

'You don't know where I live.'

'No, but you're going to give me your address.'

Marc could say no, but he had a feeling that Laurie wouldn't accept it. What was it she'd said about the gym guy not taking no for an answer? She could give the man a real run for his money. Knowing he was beaten, he gave in and scribbled his address on a piece of scrap paper.

She stuffed it in the pocket of her trousers. 'Great. By the way, depending on how much rain we get over the next couple of days, you might need wellies. It can get a bit boggy. If you don't have any, I can borrow Joe's.'

Joe—was that Izzy's father? he wondered.

The question must have been written over his face, because she explained, 'Joe's my big brother.'

'The computer expert?'

She looked pleased that he'd remembered. 'That's him.'

'I have wellies.'

'Good. I probably won't see you before the end of surgery, so have a nice day.' She smiled. 'See you on Sunday.'

Marc had no idea what he'd agreed to. And he really wasn't sure whether he was more intrigued or terrified. Whatever, Sunday was going to be *interesting...*

CHAPTER FOUR

ON SUNDAY morning, Marc was half expecting Laurie to be late, given how chaotic her house was. But she was dead on time, pulling up outside his house in an estate car—which *was* chaotic inside—with a child seat in the back containing Izzy, and a dog guard behind that so Cocoa could sit in the very back of the car without wriggling over into the back seat next to Izzy.

The little girl beamed at him as he opened the passenger door. 'Hello, Dr Bailey.'

Formality didn't sit easily with him. 'You can call me Marc, if you like,' he offered.

'Marc.' Her smile widened; she clearly loved the thought of having a grown-up friend. And Marc was torn between being charmed and wanting to back away.

'So where are we going?' he asked.

'You'll see,' Laurie said, at the same time as Izzy burst out, 'To see the bluebells!'

'Bluebells?' Marc asked.

'Just outside the next village is one of the last patches of the ancient woods of England,' Laurie explained. 'And this weekend of the year is when the bluebell carpet in the woods is at its best. They're proper English bluebells, with a scent, not the hybrids you get in stately homes and what have you. It's always packed, so we come to see them early, before the crowds get there.'

She smiled at him, and his heart actually skipped a beat. Oh, help. He didn't trust himself to say a word; all he could do was hope that she didn't think he was being rude.

'And you definitely don't get this in London, I can tell you,' she said.

When they got there, the car park, to his eyes, looked more like a bog. No wonder she'd said to bring wellington boots. But Laurie didn't seem to be bothered by the mud. She simply changed Izzy's shoes for a pair of bright red wellies, then changed her own for bright purple boots covered with large white polka dots.

Marc hid a smile. He'd known Laurie Grant for a week, but he already had a fair idea of what made her tick and he wasn't in the slightest bit surprised that she'd picked something so exuberant. They suited her right down to the ground. His own wellies were much more boring, plain and black. Which he supposed suited him, too: dull and boring.

Laurie clipped the lead onto Cocoa's collar, and the dog jumped out of the car, wagging his tail. Izzy held onto Laurie's free hand, then looked at him with a slight frown. 'This is the first time you've been here, so you might be a bit scared.'

She gave him a bright smile; she was definitely her mother's daughter, he thought.

'You can hold my other hand, if you like,' she suggested. 'That'll make you feel brave.'

Marc's first instinct was to say no. The idea of holding the little girl's hand, looking as if they were out together on a family outing—when he knew damn well he didn't *deserve* a family— made him feel slightly sick.

But then Izzy smiled at him again and something felt as if it had cracked inside him. 'Thank you. I'd love to hold your hand.' To his ears, his voice sounded rusty. He glanced at Laurie for direction—was he doing the right thing?—but she was behaving as if absolutely nothing was out of the ordinary.

Together, hand in hand, they walked through coppiced woodlands. Marc could see the odd patch of primroses, and some white flowers he vaguely recognised but didn't have a clue what their names were, but there were no bluebells.

Then Marc caught his breath as they turned the corner and he could see bluebells absolutely everywhere. He'd never seen anything like it before. Deeper into the wood, in dappled sunlight, there were more patches of deep blue. 'That's stunning,' he said. 'A real bluebell carpet.'

'Isn't it just?' Laurie said softly. 'Though I always think they look more like drifts of bluebells at the side of the path. Like blue snow. Wait until we get there and you can catch the scent.'

Marc had never seen anything so lovely—and it was so different from London. Instead of the noise of traffic, all he could hear was birds singing. He didn't have a clue what birds they were, but their songs sounded beautiful.

And then, as they drew closer, he caught the scent of the bluebells. Delicate and sweet, like a slightly softer version of a hyacinth. The epitome of a late English spring.

'So, are you glad I nagged you into this?' Laurie asked softly.

'Very,' he admitted. 'I wouldn't have missed this for the world.'

'I told you it was special.'

Yes. And so, Marc was beginning to realise, was she.

'Would you mind holding Cocoa while I take some pictures of Izzy for her grandparents?' she asked.

'Sure.' He loosened his hand from the little girl's so he could take the dog's lead from Laurie, and wasn't sure whether he felt more relieved or bereft. This whole thing was stirring up memories and dreams for him, the good mixed up with the bad and the unthinkable, all blurring into one.

'Izzy, darling, come and stand here so I can take your picture for Nanna and Granddad— remember not to squash the bluebells, so other people who come to see them can enjoy them, too,' Laurie said. She took a camera from her handbag and crouched down so she could take pictures of her daughter with the bluebells in the background. 'My parents used to do this with my brother and me every year,' she said, 'and it's lovely to look back on the pictures and see how we change from year to year.'

How his own parents would've loved a picture of their first grandchild among the bluebells, Marc thought. A little girl or a little boy in red wellington boots, just like Izzy was. He had to swallow the sudden lump in his throat. To distract himself, as much as anything else, he suggested, 'Why don't I take some pictures of you both with Cocoa?'

'Would you mind? Oh, that'd be lovely. Thank you, Marc.' Laurie's smile was sweet and piercing, widening the crack round his heart.

Marc had to hide a smile when he heard Izzy tell the dog very solemnly to be careful not to tread on the bluebells—she really was a carbon copy of her mother— but the Labrador was on his best behaviour and sat perfectly still, his mouth open as if he were smiling.

'Mummy, can you take a picture of me with Marc, please?' Izzy piped up.

Help. This wasn't what he'd signed up for. But, even though it made him feel slightly uncomfortable, he didn't have the heart to refuse to have his photograph taken with her.

Izzy insisted on seeing the photograph on the screen on the back of Laurie's camera.

'Perfect,' she said in satisfaction. 'Mummy, can we print it out and put it up in the kitchen with all the other photos? Marc's our new friend, so he should be there with everyone else.'

'Yes, darling, of course we can,' Laurie said with a smile.

Our new friend. Izzy had accepted him so easily, just as she'd clearly accepted the little girl who'd just joined her class and had made her into a friend. Marc felt a complete fraud. If either of them knew what he'd done, he was pretty sure they wouldn't want to have anything to do him.

'I'll print out a copy for you, too, Marc,' Laurie added.

'Thank you.' He hoped he didn't sound as grumpy and ungrateful to her as he did to himself. He didn't mean to be. It was just that this whole thing made him feel all mixed up again.

To his relief, once Laurie had finished taking photos, they walked on. Izzy didn't stop chattering to him, but she didn't seem to worry that Marc wasn't quite as communicative as her mother.

As they walked on, the sky was getting darker. And then Marc heard a loud rolling boom. 'Was that a plane?' he asked.

Laurie glanced up at the sky. 'No. It looks like a thunderstorm over there, and it's heading this way.' She grimaced. 'Rats. They mentioned it on the weather forecast this morning, but I hoped it would hold off until this afternoon. If we don't get back to the car before the storm reaches us, I'm afraid we're going to get a little bit wet. Sorry about that.'

'I really don't mind if we get wet,' Marc said, meaning it. 'It'll be worth it for seeing the bluebells.'

There was another rolling boom. This time, Marc timed it. 'That was eight seconds. So does that mean the storm's eight miles away?'

'No, it's one mile for every second between

seeing the flash and hearing the thunder,' Laurie explained. 'The thunder always seems to last longer out here; I guess the sound rolls around more, as the land's so flat.'

Then the first drops fell, slow but huge spatters of rain.

'We're going to have to make a run for it,' Laurie said. 'Marc, do you want to run with Cocoa or with Izzy?'

'Me!' Izzy piped up. She took Marc's hand, but with her legs being so much shorter than his she simply couldn't keep up with him as he ran.

Marc had no choice. He couldn't let the little girl get soaked or fall face first onto the boggy ground, could he? So he scooped her up and ran behind Laurie, carrying her in his arms.

Just as he would've done with his own child. If he'd had the chance.

He forced himself not to think about that and concentrated on following Laurie back to the car and not dropping Izzy.

They were all soaked by the time they got back to the car. Laurie unclipped Cocoa's lead and put him in the back while Marc helped Izzy into her seat. But the buckle defeated him. 'Sorry, I don't have a clue how these things work,' he admitted.

'You don't have any nephews or nieces?' Laurie asked.

'No, my sister's five years younger than I am and she's single,' he said, then winced, hoping that Laurie didn't think he was making a comment about her situation.

But she didn't seem in the slightest bit fazed by his words. She had the harness clipped in place within seconds. Izzy was shivering, and Laurie kissed her. 'I'll put the heater on, darling, and we'll go home now so you can change into some dry clothes. We won't be long, I promise. OK?'

'OK, Mummy.' The little girl's teeth were chattering. 'Love you.'

'Love you, too.'

Again, time seemed to shift in Marc's head. Ginny would have been exactly like this with their child—warm, loving, comforting.

If only.

Laurie drove back to her place. 'Do you mind if I get Izzy into dry clothes before I drop you home, Marc?' she asked.

'Don't worry about giving me a lift. I can walk back from here.'

Laurie frowned. 'Your place is a good couple of miles away from here. And it's still raining.'

He shrugged. 'It doesn't matter. I don't mind walking.'

'Look, if you want to stay for lunch, you're very welcome. It's nothing fancy—only soup and a sandwich, because Mum's cooking for us all tonight,' she offered.

It was so very, very tempting. But Marc couldn't let himself do it. He needed to be back at home. In safety. Where he could repair his barriers again. 'No, I'll be fine—but thanks for the offer. And thank you for taking me to see the bluebells.'

'Pleasure. But if you won't let me drop you home, at least stay until the rain dies down and have a cup of tea,' Laurie urged.

He shook his head. 'I'm already wet, so a bit more rain isn't going to make much difference. See you later. Bye, Izzy.'

'Bye, Marc!' The little girl waved madly at him.

And he was gone.

He'd bolted, Laurie thought as she helped Izzy change into dry clothes. What had scared him most, her or Izzy? He didn't seem entirely comfortable around children; and yet he'd held her little girl's hand, and carried her back to the car when it was raining. So was it her? Did he think she'd been coming on to him? OK, yes, she found him attractive—especially when she saw one of his rare smiles—but she hadn't intended to do anything about it. Had she been giving out the wrong signals?

Marc Bailey was a puzzle. And she didn't have a clue how to start working him out.

Laurie didn't see Marc at the surgery on the Monday or Tuesday, but on Wednesday he left an email for her on the surgery system: *Can we have a project update this evening?*

Sure. What time? she typed back, sent the message, and called in her next patient.

When she was writing up her notes after the consultation, her computer beeped to signal a message from someone in the practice. Marc again: *Is 8 OK?*

8 is fine, she replied. Izzy would be in bed,

asleep, so they'd be able to get everything sorted without interruptions. But she also wondered whether maybe Marc was avoiding the little girl, too, given the way he'd dashed off on Sunday.

'Focus on your work. On your patients. Whatever issues Marc Bailey has, they're none of your business,' she told herself sharply.

All the same, she couldn't help wondering.

Marc was perfectly polite when he turned up at her house at exactly eight o'clock. But he also threw her by giving her a huge bunch of glorious red tulips.

'Oh—how lovely! Thank you.'

'These are to say thank you for Sunday,' Marc said. 'And because I feel guilty that you've been the one doing all the hospitality—you've supplied all the cake and the coffee.'

'Only because it's easier for me if we meet here. And it's been costing you petrol,' she pointed out, hoping that she didn't sound as flustered as she felt.

When was the last time someone had bought her flowers, other than her parents or her brother?

Though he hadn't given them to her in a romantic sense, she reminded herself crossly. This wasn't a date. This was work. He was just being polite.

But it still flustered her. Especially because she loved the glossy showiness of the flowers; they were exactly the sort of thing she'd buy herself as a treat at the end of a hard week.

'Come through into the kitchen and sit down. I'm going to put these gorgeous flowers in water before we start.'

She put the tulips in a vase of water, placed them on the kitchen windowsill, then made them both a coffee and sat down at the kitchen table with him. 'All righty. Jay—my friend at the university—is letting me have twenty monitors. We have a diabetic expert, a nutritionist and a cardiologist who've agreed to do a talk for us, and we've got the village hall for an hour at eight on Wednesday evenings.'

'We have ten yeses so far,' he said, taking out a folder to show her the replies they'd received. 'I'll give it until Friday and then, if we still have fewer than twenty, I'll start ringing round and talking them into filling up the spaces.'

'Great. We can always spread the monitoring, if anyone else wants to join in a bit later,' she said. 'What about our exercise providers?'

They worked through their list, and within forty minutes had worked out a schedule including badminton, ballroom dancing, martial arts and circuit training, as well as toning exercise.

'Obviously the swimming and the aqua aerobics will have to be at the pool,' she said, 'and the walking group is obviously going to be outdoors, but we've got a good mix over the next three or four months.' She smiled at him. 'Thanks for all your help on this. It would've taken me ages to do everything on my own.'

'No problem. And you'll be pleased to know that Neil Peascod wasn't, um, persistent with me.'

'Funny guy.' But she liked the fact that Marc was teasing her. It meant he felt more confident in her company, and maybe that he felt accepted as part of the team at the practice. 'I'm glad you came round this evening.'

Marc went very still. She'd wanted to see him? Why? 'Oh?' he asked carefully.

'Because I was wondering if I was a problem for you.'

Oh, no. Please don't let her be that perceptive. 'How do you mean?' he asked.

'On Sunday,' she said, 'you couldn't wait to leave. I wasn't sure if the problem was me or Izzy but I figured that, as you held her hand in the woods and you carried her back to the car, it was probably me.'

He blew out a breath. 'No, it's not you. It's me.'

'I'm guessing,' she said softly, 'that you came to Norfolk to get away from London—and you left someone special behind.'

Yes, he had. But not quite in the way she was obviously thinking.

'Divorce is always hard, even if it's amicable— and most of the time it's not that,' she said. 'But it does get better. Or, at least, easier to comes to terms with, in time.'

'You think I'm divorced?'

She shrugged. 'You have a white line on the ring finger of your left hand.'

Yes, because he'd taken off his wedding ring the day before he'd moved out of London, in an attempt to try to move on.

'I used to have one of those myself,' she said.

'I'm not divorced.' There was a lump in his throat, but he needed to get the words out. To stop Laurie making any more assumptions. He owed her at least some of the truth. 'My wife died.'

She reached over the table to squeeze his hand. 'I'm sorry, Marc. That's rough on you, to lose your wife so young.'

She didn't know the half of it. All of a sudden, it was too much for him and he couldn't handle it. 'It was all my fault,' he said tonelessly. And then, because there was nothing else he could say, and he couldn't bear to sit there being polite over coffee when all he wanted to do was curl into a ball and howl at the memories filling his head, he pushed his chair back and walked out.

Laurie stared after him, too stunned to call him back.

How could his wife's death possibly be Marc's fault? No way could she believe that. Marc Bailey was a good GP; she'd heard on the grapevine that their patients were more than happy with him. And he'd been good with Izzy, letting her chatter on to him and not cutting her off impatiently.

No way could a man like that be to blame for anyone's death.

Poor guy. She'd made assumptions, jumped in with both feet and pushed him way too far.

They needed to talk. Sooner, rather than later. But she couldn't leave Izzy alone in the house, and this wasn't the sort of conversation you could have on the phone or by text. So she'd have to leave it until tomorrow.

But there was one thing she knew always made people feel better. Something that helped them to talk. 'We have work to do,' she told Cocoa, and got out the ingredients to make one of her lemon cakes.

CHAPTER FIVE

LAURIE walked into her consulting room the next morning with a tin of cake, intending to tackle Marc and sort things out between them before he saw his first patient. But she stopped when she saw a square box on her desk, neatly wrapped and tied with a ribbon; an envelope was sticking out from the parcel.

Who would leave something like this on her desk? It wasn't her birthday and it couldn't be a present from a grateful patient; Phyllis would've explained to anyone who'd brought in a gift that medics weren't allowed to accept anything from patients, but a communal jar of coffee for the practice kitchen or a donation to their charity of the month instead would be very much appreciated.

Surprised, Laurie opened the envelope, read the note swiftly, and realised that Marc had beaten her to it.

Sorry. I shouldn't have said what I did last night. Can we talk, please? M

He had bold, confident handwriting—and yet Laurie was pretty sure that, deep inside, Marc was neither. He was torturing himself, and although he'd left London behind he clearly hadn't been able to leave his demons there.

Laurie hadn't slept well last night, unable to stop thinking about what he'd told her. Any attempt to guess at what he'd actually meant would've been wild speculation, because she didn't have a clue, but one thing she was convinced about was that he was punishing himself unnecessarily.

She untied the ribbon and removed the wrapping paper. The box contained a gorgeous selection of chocolates—expensive ones, she recognised. To get them on her desk this morning before her shift, Marc would've had to make a special trip to the supermarket five miles down the road to buy them.

He'd made a real effort.

Now it was time for her to do the same. She picked up the phone and dialled his extension.

He answered on the second ring. 'Marc Bailey.'

'Marc, it's Laurie.' She paused. 'You really didn't have to buy me chocolates, you know.'

'I did, actually, because I felt bad. It's an apology. I shouldn't have said what I did and walked out on you. It really wasn't fair to dump that on you. And I'm sorry.'

'It was my own fault, for pushing you too hard. And I'm sorry for that. So let's call it quits.' She paused. 'I feel horribly guilty about taking these posh chocolates.'

'They're for *you*, Laurie. Not for the surgery,' he said quietly.

She knew what he meant. If she put them on the table in the staff kitchen, everyone in the practice would start speculating about who had bought Laurie a gift like that. In a small town, secrets didn't stay secret for very long; they'd soon find out that he was the one who'd bought them. And the last thing Marc needed was people talking about him. Given that he was a widower at such a young age, he'd probably had more than enough pity and sympathy at his last practice. That was probably why he'd moved here, she realised: to make a new start. Where there weren't any memories and wouldn't be any unwanted pity.

'You really didn't have to buy them, but thank you,' she said softly.

'Can we start again?' he asked carefully.

'Of course we can. Actually, I made you a cake as a peace offering.'

He gave a wry chuckle. 'You fix everything by cake, don't you?'

'Don't knock it. Cake goes a long way towards fixing an awful lot of things.' She paused, and decided to take a risk. 'Do you want to grab a sandwich from the patisserie at lunchtime with me and eat it by the duck pond?'

'That'd be good.'

'I only get twenty minutes for lunch,' she warned. 'Because I'm part time, I have paperwork to do and then I'm on phone triage before I take Cocoa out and pick Izzy up from school.'

'I'll make sure I'm on time,' he promised.

'Good. I'll leave the cake in the staffroom, then. Sam will think I made it for him, and we won't disillusion him.'

'Agreed. And thank you,' he said softly.

* * *

It was a busy morning at the practice, but both Marc and Laurie finished their surgeries on time.

She smiled at him. 'Right. Time to introduce you to my favourite bad habit—as in the best bread I've ever tasted.' She took him to the patisserie in the middle of the high street.

'Let me see. It's Thursday. So would that be a sweet chilli chicken salad wrap and a bottle of sparkling water to go, Dr Grant?' the woman behind the counter asked Laurie with a grin.

'I might just have the special today, Tina,' Laurie said.

Tina just snorted. 'Yeah, right, Laurie. Any day with a Y in it, you order a sweet chilli chicken salad wrap.'

'Tut. And just when I was going to introduce a new customer to you,' Laurie teased. 'You'll put him off.'

Tina just laughed. 'He'll be just like everyone else—one taste of my mum's bread, and you're hooked.' She smiled at Marc. 'Hi. I'm Tina. Nice to meet you.'

His answering smile was slightly wary. 'Marc Bailey.'

'My new colleague,' Laurie added. 'So be nice, Tina.'

'I'm *always* nice. What can I get you, Marc?'

He looked slightly lost. 'Um—what do you recommend?'

'Are you a vegetarian?'

'No, I eat most things.'

'Crab salad, then,' Tina said. 'The fish man was here this morning, and they were freshly caught at Cromer. And a strawberry tartlet— Karl brought in the first batch from the new season's crop this morning, so I couldn't resist making them, and my pastry is much better than *hers*.' She indicated Laurie.

'But *my* lemon cake trumps *hers*. By miles,' Laurie retorted.

'In your dreams, sweetie.' Tina sorted out their order. 'Laurie, Georgia's been plotting play dates with Izzy. Is it OK with you if she comes over for tea and a play at our place after school on Monday?'

'She did say something about that to me the other day, so I'm sure she'd love to,' Laurie said.

'And she's been talking about Molly, the new girl.'

'So has Georgia.' Tina smiled. 'I'll catch Molly's mum in the playground today and see if Molly can come, too. But either way I'll pick Izzy up from school for you on Monday.'

'Thanks. And how about I pick Georgia up the Monday after, for tea and a play at ours?' Laurie said. 'And if you see Molly's mum before I do, invite her to mine that day as well.'

'Will do.' Tina finished wrapping their sandwiches for them and took the money. 'Catch you at school this afternoon.'

'So they know you pretty well at the patisserie, then?' Marc asked when he and Laurie were settled on the bench by the duck pond.

'I grew up here, so I went to school with some of the staff,' she said. 'We lost touch a bit when I went to university, but I've got to know some of them better in the playground while we're waiting to pick up the kids from school. You've probably already worked out that Tina's daughter Georgia is Izzy's best friend—and, although Tina teases me like mad, we get on really well, too.' She smiled. 'I've been really lucky in that everyone's accepted me back here for who I am. Nobody's given me a hard time for making a mess of things in London.'

Laurie was a bit chaotic, Marc knew, but that wasn't the same as making a mess of things. 'I can't imagine you making a mess of things.'

'Don't you believe it.' She gave him a wry look. 'There's my relationship, for starters. I'm usually a pretty good judge of character, but Dean sneaked under my radar. Looking back, I should never have gone out with him, let alone got engaged to him and bought a house with him.'

'It's easy to be wise in hindsight.' Marc surprised himself by asking, 'Was the break-up a long time ago?'

'It probably started the day I did a positive pregnancy test,' she said. 'But, for all I know, there could've been other affairs before then.'

He blinked. 'Your fiancé had an affair?'

'He was with a patient when I was in labour with Izzy.' She paused. 'That's not as in treating an emergency, by the way, because he's a dermatologist. That's *with* with.'

He blew out a breath. Was the man crazy? Why on earth would he cheat on a woman like Laurie? 'I don't know what to say.'

Her smile held no mirth whatsoever. 'Most people have plenty to say. Starting with Dean being a cheating scumbag and me being an idiot for not spotting how unreliable he was. But he wasn't really a scumbag.'

'No?' Marc couldn't help the question.

'No. He just didn't do responsibility. It was different at work—he's really good at his job and he'd never, ever let a patient or a colleague down—but he couldn't cope with responsibility at home. He left everything to me to deal with.' She shrugged. 'I should've worked that out for myself and not expected more from him than he was able to give.'

'That's very forgiving of you.'

'I wasn't very forgiving at the time. I left him, because no way was I going to let him cheat on me again.' She bit her lip. 'And the one thing I still can't forgive him for is the fact that he hasn't seen Izzy since the day I left him. When she was a week old and I found out about his affair. He's never shown the slightest bit of interest in her, and in the few days when we both lived with him, he never once changed her nappy or offered to give her a bath, and he certainly didn't make a move towards her if she cried. It was as if she didn't even exist.' She sighed. 'OK, Izzy wasn't actually planned, but it takes two to make a baby. She's his *daughter*. And I really don't understand how he could ignore her.'

'I take it he wasn't happy about you being pregnant, then?'

'You could say that. When we found out that I was pregnant, he suggested that I could have a termination.' Her voice was dry.

Marc felt anger surge through him. Whatever was wrong with the man? The day he and Ginny had found out that she was pregnant had been one of the happiest of his life. With the injury to his shoulder, he hadn't been able to pick his wife up and whirl her round in joy, but he'd bought his wife the biggest bouquet of flowers that the florist could arrange for him. And he'd made sure Ginny had felt loved and supported all the way. He'd been overjoyed at the idea of making a family together.

And then he'd wrecked it all with his self-ishness.

Which, he supposed, really made him no better than Laurie's ex.

Laurie didn't seem to read anything into his silence, and he guessed that most people reacted the same way. Anger, disbelief, and not having a clue what to say.

'Dean just doesn't want to be a father,' she said. 'Which is ironic, really, as Izzy has at least two half-siblings—to my knowledge, anyway.'

'Two?' Marc didn't follow. If the man had wanted Laurie to have a termination, how come he'd gone on to have two more children?

'Neither of them were planned. One of them was the patient he was, um, *with* when I was in labour. When that came out, he had to pass her case to a colleague. And then he did the same to her as he had to me. The second he found out she was pregnant, he lost interest in her and started seeing someone else.' Laurie shook her head. 'It's weird, really, because his parents are ever so nice and they're still involved in Izzy's life. He really can't blame the way he is on having a dysfunctional upbringing.' She shrugged.

'Or maybe his parents gave him a bit too much. He was an only child, they had him quite late in life, and maybe they wrapped him more in cotton wool than the average parent would've done.'

'You mean, they spoiled him.'

'Sort of, but when they found out why I'd left him they didn't try to pin the blame on me or make any feeble excuses for his behaviour. They were really angry with him and threatened to disown him. I had to persuade them out of it.'

'That's very forgiving of you,' he said again. 'I'm not sure I could've done that, in your shoes.' Forgiveness was a tricky thing. He couldn't forgive himself. Ginny's parents couldn't forgive him either. And he knew that they were right. He should've taken better care of his wife and their unborn child.

'Dean's their only child. Expecting them to cut him out of their life because he'd made a bad decision—well, that wouldn't be fair on them. What he really needs is a good shake and to learn to face up to responsibility. And to learn how to make a proper commitment to someone.'

'Would you take him back if he did?'

She shook her head. 'I don't love him any more.

We did have some good times, and I'll always be grateful that he gave me Izzy, but it wouldn't work out between us now. And I'm really glad I didn't marry him. It was a bit of a mess to sort out the house, but it would've dragged on much longer if we'd had to go through a divorce as well.' She sighed. 'I feel so sorry for his parents, because Izzy's the only one of their grandchildren that they actually see. They live the other side of the country, so they don't see Iz as often as they'd like to, but I email photographs to them every week—like the ones I took at the bluebell woods—and she draws them pictures so they don't feel completely left out.'

'I'm impressed that you're so—well, balanced about it.'

'It wasn't their fault that I broke off my engagement to their son, and you're not meant to be impressed.' She ate a bite of her sandwich. 'Life's very short, and what's the point of making things harder than they need to be, or hurting people? I don't want Izzy growing up seeing only the dark side of things and the negatives. Sure, not everything in life is going to work out absolutely perfectly, but you can always make the best of what you have.'

Pollyanna. And, given what she'd just told him, he could understand her needing that kind of defence mechanism. To see the best in things and block out the bad stuff, at least in front of her daughter.

'You're a fixer, aren't you?' he asked. He knew she was doing exactly that with him. Taking him under her wing, because he was a newcomer to the area and didn't know anyone. Just the same as when she and Tina had been planning a play date for their children and they'd included the new little girl Izzy had talked about.

'It's why I'm a doctor.' She looked at him. 'And why you are, too, I'd guess.'

He sighed. 'Yeah. Though I couldn't fix the one important thing.' And he definitely couldn't tell her the whole of it, especially after what she'd just told him. He had a nasty feeling that she'd think as badly of him as she thought of her ex.

'For what it's worth,' she said softly, 'I don't believe a word of what you said last night. You're a good man. You've gone above and beyond the call of duty with my pet project, you've been patient with Izzy even though close contact with children obviously isn't comfortable for you, and our patients think you're the best thing since sliced bread. And that really doesn't fit with what you're accusing yourself of.'

He shifted awkwardly on the wooden bench. 'I guess I owe it to you to tell you the truth.'

'You don't owe me anything, Marc,' she corrected. 'But if you want to talk to me, I'll listen and it won't go any further than me.'

'Thank you.'

Though he couldn't get the words to come out. He couldn't frame them in the right way. He knew she was going to think badly of him when she knew the truth. OK, so it was his just deserts; but he *liked* Laurie and he didn't want her to despise him.

Then again, the truth would come out eventually. It was better that she heard it from him, and better that she knew sooner rather than later.

'That rugby accident I told you about—I didn't cope very well with it,' he began.

'Not many people would. A rotator cuff tear is pretty painful.'

'Yes, but what I hated was not being able to move easily, not being able to do everything I'd always taken for granted, and having to rely on other people to do things for me. I couldn't play the game I'd loved since I was a kid, and watching it...' He grimaced. 'That was a really poor second best. When you watch a match, it's nowhere near the same as the buzz you get from playing in it. And I hated the fact I'd let the team down.'

'It wasn't your fault that you got injured—and, to be honest, you know it's a "when" rather than an "if" that you're going to get injured when you play contact sports,' she reminded him.

'I still felt I'd let the team down. And it was even worse when I realised how much damage I'd done to my shoulder—it wasn't just that I'd be out for the rest of the season. I was never going to play again.'

'Couldn't you have switched to, I dunno, coaching or something?' she asked.

'Not properly—talking someone through a move isn't always enough, and showing someone how to do something would've risked more damage to my shoulder.' He sighed. 'Work was bad, too. With my arm out of action, I couldn't even examine patients properly. The only thing I could do until I was healed was phone triage.' He grimaced. 'I could manage a phone, as long as it was on loudspeaker, and I could type up my notes one-handed, but I didn't feel I was doing a proper doctor's job.'

'Phone triage isn't so bad,' she said. 'You get to reassure people, and that's worth something.'

Still seeing the positive, Marc thought. He hadn't been able to see that kind of positive in his job; at the time, he'd only been able to focus on what he hadn't been able to do. 'When it's for a morning a week, as part of a rota, triage is OK—but when it's the only thing you can do, it's unbearable.'

'Was it the shoulder of your writing hand that you damaged?' she asked.

'No, my left. Which is my gear-changing hand, and my car's manual rather than automatic, so I couldn't drive either.' He grimaced. 'I was disgustingly sorry for myself and I behaved really badly. I started drinking a bit too much in an effort to cope with it—and when that didn't work, I drank more to blot out how I felt.'

She said nothing and there was no censure in her gorgeous blue eyes, but Marc still found himself squirming.

'I can understand why people drink too much, now I've done it myself,' he said. 'I didn't actually become an alcoholic but, looking back, I can see I could've gone down that road so very easily.'

Had it not been for the accident. That had stopped him in his tracks. He hadn't touched a drop of alcohol since.

His mouth went dry again. 'My wife… We lived in London, so Ginny hadn't bothered learning to drive. There was no real need, with public transport being so good. But we'd thought about moving out of London, so that would've meant not having such good public transport and needing to drive, so she decided to have lessons. She passed her driving test a couple of weeks before my accident. I'm not one of these men who can't stand to be driven by a woman, and I was glad that she had a chance to get more experience driving because I was out of action, but…' He shook his head. 'I leaned on her too much.'

'If you couldn't drive, what else was she supposed to do? Let you struggle? Make you change the car for an automatic?'

Fair point, he thought. But Laurie still didn't get it. So he had to be honest with her. Tell her the worst. 'We went to a party. My arm was better by then, so I was supposed to be driving us home. But, as I said, I'd got into the habit of drinking. I had two or three glasses of wine without even thinking about it. Then I realised I was over the limit, so Ginny was going to have to drive us home.'

'She hadn't been drinking, too?' Laurie asked.

'No.' Because of the baby. But he couldn't quite bring himself to tell Laurie that. 'On the way back, we collided with another car. It wasn't Ginny's fault—it was the other driver's. He was concentrating on his mobile phone instead of where he was going, and his car was on the wrong side of the road.' Marc closed his eyes. 'She didn't even have time to beep her horn at him to warn him we were there. She drove round the corner and he was just there, heading straight for us.' His breath hitched. 'And I got out of that car without a single scratch. No bruising, no blood, no whiplash, nothing. But Ginny… Her side of the car took the brunt of the impact. She was killed instantly.'

Along with their baby. His whole life had shattered like the windscreen of their car.

Laurie took his hand. 'I'm so sorry. But, Marc, you weren't to blame. The other driver was on the wrong side of the road.'

'But if I hadn't been so selfish, so self-indulgent, and drunk too much, I would've been driving, like I was supposed to. Maybe we would've gone home by a different route. Maybe we would've gone home at a different time. Maybe I could've avoided the accident.'

'That's a lot of maybes,' Laurie said. 'And has it occurred to you that maybe if you had been driving, you would've been the one killed in the crash and Ginny would've been left to cope on her own?'

Yes. But it hadn't made him feel any better. 'It was my fault,' he repeated.

'Tell me,' she said softly, 'if a patient told you what you've just told me, would you be blaming him for his wife's death?'

'I…' He shook his head. This was too close to the bone. 'I can't answer that. I don't know.'

'I don't think you would. I think you'd be telling your patient that it was an accident—that it was something outside his control and it wasn't fair to beat himself up over it.'

'Maybe. But I can't forgive myself, Laurie. And neither can her parents. I let her down. And I hate myself for what I did.'

'When did it happen?' she asked softly.

'Two years ago.'

'That's a long, long time to hate yourself.'

He sighed. 'I know. I did try counselling, but…' He shrugged. 'Maybe I just wasn't a good fit with that particular guy and someone else could've made me see things differently. But he told me that I was the only one who could forgive myself, and I'd have to come to terms with it in my own time.'

'He sounds like our awful ex-locum,' she said. 'Yes, you *are* the only one who can forgive yourself; but counsellors are supposed to help you find the tools to do that. He clearly didn't.' She squeezed his hand. 'I'm not going to patronise you or tell you what to do. But what I can tell you is that our patients like you and you really fit in at the practice. Sam would never have offered you the job if he thought you wouldn't take proper care with the patients. And all that means you're a better man than you think you are.'

'Maybe.'

'Definitely.' She glanced at his sandwich. 'If you've finished with that, I know some ducks that'd be very interested in the crusts.'

Feeding the ducks. Something he'd been looking forward to doing with his child. How could he do this now?

But Laurie had saved bits of her wrap for the ducks, and it seemed churlish not to join her. Especially as she hadn't judged him anywhere near as harshly as he deserved.

And Marc discovered that, actually, feeding the ducks on a sunny lunchtime was fun, watching them splashing and diving for the scraps of bread.

'I do this with Iz on Saturday mornings,' she said. 'We buy a couple of rolls from the patisserie, especially to feed the ducks. Though don't tell Tina or I'll be toast.' She paused. 'You're welcome to join us this weekend, if you like.'

'Thanks, but...' He couldn't think of an excuse, and just gave her an awkward smile.

'I knew you'd say that.' She spread her hands. 'Well, it's an open invitation. If you change your mind, that's fine. Just call me on Saturday morning and I'll tell you what time we're going to be here. Oh, and you'd better eat that strawberry tart, because Tina's going to ask you what you thought of it next time she sees you.'

'She is?'

'And not necessarily in the patisserie. You'll probably bump into her in town at some point, and she'll ask you then.'

He looked at her. 'People actually do that?'

'Welcome to life in a small town, Dr Bailey,' she said with a grin. 'I assume you've only ever lived in a city?'

'London,' he confirmed. 'I grew up there, I trained there, and I worked there.'

'London. Where nobody really gets the chance to know anyone. It's very different here.'

Marc wasn't sure if it was a promise or a warning. He'd spent the last two years keeping himself separate—keeping himself sane. And it seemed that it was going to be much harder to do that here. That he was going to be part of the community, whether he liked it or not. In London, he'd never so much as seen his patients outside work. Here, he was living among them.

She smiled at him. 'I'd better get back to my paperwork. It's up to you if you want to stay and talk to the ducks for a bit or if you want to come back to the practice with me.'

Again, there was no censure in her face, no judgement. Just her down-to-earth smile and good humour. He glanced at his watch. 'I'll stay with the ducks.' Try to get his head back together. 'But thank you, Laurie. For listening.'

'No worries. And it's not going any further than me,' she reassured him. 'See you later.'

CHAPTER SIX

LAURIE wasn't too surprised that Marc didn't ring her on Saturday or join her with Izzy in feeding the ducks. Now he'd told her about the accident, he was probably worrying that she'd judge him and find him wanting as a human being. Apart from the fact it wasn't true, she thought that Marc had already done more than enough judging of himself. Unfairly so.

She didn't really get to see him until their first session with their patients on the following Wednesday evening. She wasn't sure whether Marc was actively avoiding her or just busy. In the end, she'd had to resort to using the surgery email to ask him if he wanted to do the talk to the patients at the surgery on Wednesday evening.

It's your project, so I'm happy for you to do it, if you want to. I'll give you whatever support you need. M

It was nice that he wasn't trying to take charge, the way Dean probably would've done if she'd worked on a project with him. Even so, Laurie had the distinct feeling that Marc was avoiding her—and she had a pretty good idea why, too. Because she knew the truth about him.

How could she make him see that it hadn't changed anything? The past was the past. It had been a tragic accident. And he was being totally unfair to himself.

Laurie was already in the surgery waiting room at half past seven when Marc arrived.

'Hi, there.' She looked up from one of the chairs she was rearranging.

'Leave that. Let me do the heavy stuff,' he said.

She raised an eyebrow. 'You mean a mere woman can't move a chair?'

'A woman's perfectly capable of moving a chair,' he said, 'but it makes sense for the person with the bigger muscles to lift the heavier stuff, whether that person's male or female.'

She grinned. 'OK. I'm pleased to say that you've just passed the sexism test, Dr Bailey.'

'Good. What do you want done and where?'

'Chairs there, and a couple of tables—one at the front for the speakers, and one for refreshments, please.' She looked at him. 'I'll be in the kitchen.'

'Where you'll make much better tea than I do. Ginny always says that mine's too strong.' And then he caught himself. Using the present tense again. Would he ever get used to it?

But Laurie didn't make a comment. She just smiled at him. 'I didn't make any cake for tonight. I thought it might be a bit tactless, given that we're talking about weight loss and sensible choices.'

'Fair point,' he said, and made himself smile back. 'Where's Izzy?'

'In bed. It'd be way too late for her to stay up if she came with me, especially as she's got school tomorrow.'

Of course. Why hadn't he thought of that? Probably because he wasn't used to children. And he'd avoided them in the last couple of years.

'Not to mention being incredibly boring for her, even if I'd brought pens and paper. Mum's babysitting for me,' she said. 'She's going to babysit for me on Wednesday nights during the project, so I can come along to the sessions. And I'm going to treat her to a spa day at the weekend to say thank you.'

Clearly Laurie was close to her mother, just as Ginny had been close to her parents. Marc was guiltily aware that he'd put a huge distance between himself and his own parents since the accident. Moving out of London had been just another step in that direction. Maybe he'd call them tonight when he got home. Just to say hello and let them know that he'd settled OK.

By the time he and Laurie had finished sorting things out, their speakers had arrived.

Laurie greeted Mike the cardiologist, Sally the diabetes expert and Lisa the dietician with a formal handshake and a warm smile, before introducing Marc to them; but Marc noticed that Jay, the guy in charge of the exercise project at the university, received a warm hug.

Marc was shocked and surprised to feel jealousy prickling down his spine. This was ridiculous. He didn't have the right to be jealous. He wasn't in any kind of relationship with Laurie.

She'd simply taken him under her wing because she was a fixer, and he'd be stupid to think it could be anything more than that. She'd made it very clear that she wasn't in the market for a relationship. Maybe, Marc thought, that was because she was already in a relationship. With Jay. 'Friend' had probably been an understatement.

He switched into professional mode; as the patients arrived, he helped serve coffee and tea. Laurie gave a brief talk, introducing the experts, and then let them do the rest of the talking.

Jay talked about his research and how to use the monitor—using Laurie as his model to show exactly how to wear it, Marc noted wryly. 'You'll be wearing it for a week. I'll use the numbers to show the range of results in my research, so nobody will be able to identify any of you personally from my report. But I'll also be able to give you all a personal profile so you can see for yourselves exactly how much activity you do and when,' Jay explained. 'That'll help you see where you have an opportunity to add in some exercise, or maybe change the way you do some things.'

The cardiologist, the diabetes expert and the

dietician did their talks, and Marc could see from the expressions on everyone's faces that they were all much more motivated to look at their lifestyles and see where they could make changes. Laurie's pet project was getting off to a great start. And when she handed out the schedule for the exercise taster sessions, there was a real buzz in the room as everyone discussed the options and the things they'd never even thought about trying before.

He slipped out quietly into the kitchen and sorted out the washing-up, while Laurie saw the patients out and said goodbye to the experts.

She came in when he was putting everything away.

'Oh, Marc, I'm sorry. I didn't mean to leave it all to you. You should've waited for me so I could do my fair share.'

'It's not a problem. Did your friend get off OK?' He hoped he sounded more casual than he felt.

'Jay, you mean?' She smiled. 'Yes. It's a shame they couldn't get a babysitter, or Fiona would've come too. His wife's my best friend from university. She met Jay after we graduated, and by lucky chance she ended up moving here with him, which means I get to see her a lot more often than we did just after we qualified. He's a nice guy, a real sweetheart—it's not just surface charm.'

The way it had been with her ex? Marc thought, reading between the lines.

'I think our patients liked him, too. And they were all chatting about the project as they went out, sounding really keen and enthusiastic.' She beamed at him. 'You know, I think this really might make a difference, Marc. The ones who've been struggling with their weight, the ones who are heading towards a higher risk of a heart attack or stroke and developing insulin resistance or even diabetes—we're giving them a real chance to do something about it and change their lives for the better.'

'Yes.' And now Marc felt a total fool, not just for that unexpected surge of jealousy but because it had been totally unnecessary in the first place.

'Thanks so much for your help on this. I would say let's go to the pub and I'll buy you a drink, but I guess you might not want to do that.' She squirmed. 'Sorry, that was really tactless. I didn't mean to put my foot in it.'

'You didn't. It's OK,' he reassured her. 'You guessed right: I don't drink now. Though you don't necessarily have to have alcohol in a pub.'

She brightened. 'So you'll let me buy you an orange juice or whatever in the King's Arms?'

He really ought to make an excuse. But his mouth had other ideas. 'Or you could have a coffee at my place, seeing as you've provided all the hospitality so far.'

'You're actually inviting me into the bat cave?' She slapped a hand over her mouth. 'Sorry, sorry, sorry. I can't even use a sugar rush as an excuse for letting my mouth run away with me, because there was no cake tonight. I apologise.'

The bat cave. Marc felt something bubbling inside him he hadn't felt for heaven only knew how long—laughter—and it felt good to let it out. It sounded rusty, but he was actually laughing.

Oh, wow.

Marc had only ever given Laurie the most guarded smiles before, even when they'd gone to see the bluebells. And now, seeing him laugh was a revelation. It made him look younger, much more approachable—maybe more like the man he'd been before his life had imploded in tragedy.

He was utterly, utterly gorgeous, and his mouth was beautiful. Laurie went hot as she caught her thoughts and realised she was actually wondering what that mouth would feel like on her skin. Oh, help. This was the last thing he needed. And she ought to make some excuse to put some distance between them.

Yet he'd invited her back for coffee. She guessed it was the first overture he'd made in a long, long time. Maybe even since the accident. So how could she possibly knock him back now?

'The bat cave.' He was still smiling.

'I've only seen your house from the outside,' she reminded him. 'It could be a bat cave inside.'

'I'll have you know, my house is spotless. No cobwebs, no spiders, no damp, and definitely no bats.' His eyes crinkled at the corners. 'And my coffee's excellent.'

'Sounds good to me.' She gave him a bright smile. And please let her common sense come back. Some time between right now and when they arrived at his place would be perfect.

Between them, they set the alarm on the surgery and locked up. She climbed into her car and followed Marc back to his place.

It was a beautiful old detached flint cottage, the kind of place she would've loved but couldn't afford—which was why she'd bought a modern townhouse on the new estate at the other side of the town.

'It's a lovely house,' she said as he opened the front door and ushered her inside.

'It's rented for six months,' he said. 'But I'll see how it goes. I might get a chance to buy it later.'

Meaning once he'd settled in.

And if he decided to stay. Laurie knew that his contract was initially for six months, and then he and Sam would agree on whether he'd stay with the practice or not.

She wasn't surprised that the décor inside was neutral. It was also very, very neat and tidy; again, that was understandable as it wasn't his own place. And yet there was nothing personal

about it, nothing to give her a clue about who
Marc was outside work.

She followed him into the kitchen. It was so
different from her own kitchen: no important
letters from school pinned to a cork board, and
no photographs or children's drawings held to
the fridge with magnets. It looked like a show
home, a place that would be photographed in
one of the glossy home and lifestyle magazines
she'd used to read in the days before Izzy and
Cocoa—the days when a pale carpet and white
furniture wouldn't have been totally impractical.

And there was one other big difference. The
worktops were totally clear, apart from a gleam-
ing and very expensive-looking coffee machine.
So it hadn't been an idle boast when he'd said his
coffee was excellent. Oh, help. And she'd given
him ordinary instant coffee from a jar. Which
was about the worst thing you could do to someone who was fussy about coffee.

'Proper coffee or decaf?' he asked.

'At this time of night, decaf, please—otherwise I'll be awake all night and yawning all over
my patients tomorrow.'

'Sure.' He made them both a mug of coffee as

expertly as any trained barista in a posh coffee shop. He even heated the milk and made a little pattern on top of the coffee, she noticed. A million miles away from her usual routine of pouring boiling water onto granules and sloshing in a bit of milk.

'Thank you.' She took a sip. 'This is really lovely. I think I should apologise now for giving you bog-standard instant coffee at my place.'

He smiled. 'It's OK. I'm not a coffee snob.'

'With a machine like that?' she scoffed. No way did she believe him.

'Busted, hmm?' His smile was tinged with sadness. 'Yes, well. I've learned that there are more important things in life than decent coffee.'

'Mmm.' She didn't have a clue what to say. And giving him a hug didn't seem appropriate.

'Let's go and sit down.'

The living room was just as neat as the kitchen. And just as clear. No pictures, no photographs, no books or music or films. Though, she supposed, he might keep everything as a digital copy. Less cluttered. Marc Bailey definitely wouldn't put up with the kind of chaos she lived in.

He gestured to her to sit down on the sofa, and took a seat next to her.

'So, have you settled in OK?' she asked brightly.

'More or less.' He glanced round the room and sighed. 'Well, I haven't finished unpacking.'

She could guess why, but she knew he needed space. So she waited.

'To be honest, I really can't face it,' he said. 'There are boxes in the dining room that I haven't even touched since the day the removal people packed them. I only really did the boxes for the kitchen and the bathroom. My sister Yvonne offered to come down from Glasgow to give me a hand, but I told her I was fine.'

'And you regret it now?'

'I was too proud,' he admitted. 'And I don't want to ask her now, because then she'll think…'

That there was a problem. He didn't have to say it. Particularly as there *was* a problem. Boxes filled with stuff that held too many memories for him.

'Sometimes,' she said gently, 'it's easier if someone who doesn't have any emotional involvement with the situation helps you. I don't mean to be pushy, and I won't be offended if you say no—but if you want a hand unpacking, I'd be happy to help you.'

'Dr Fixit?' he asked wryly.

'Absolutely. Plus, what goes around comes around.' She shrugged. 'My family and my friends all pitched in when I moved. Part of me wanted to be super-independent and tell everyone I could do it all on my own, but I had Izzy to think about. Also, physically, I wasn't really up to the job. I had a bit of a rough labour and I ended up with a C-section. I couldn't drive anywhere for a month afterwards or lift anything heavier than the baby. For her sake, I had to admit to my limits and accept help.'

She'd had a baby to think about. Unlike him. He just had the yawning gap of might-have-beens.

'Mum and Dad said straight away that I could stay with them while I was sorting myself out. And I really appreciated it. After Dean agreed to buy out my share of the house in London, when I bought my place, everyone pitched in again to help me move in and build the flat-pack furniture and what have you. But I grew up here, so

I know everyone. You don't, yet.' She paused. 'But if you let them close, people will be there for you.'

That was the problem. The idea of letting people close again—and then maybe letting them down...

No. 'I don't des—' he began.

She put her mug of coffee down, reached across and pressed her finger against his lips to stop the word coming out. Every nerve-end tingled where she touched him.

'Yes, you do,' she said softly. 'Everyone deserves a second chance.'

If only he could believe that.

Right now, he felt more lost and confused than he ever had in his life. And he was horribly aware of the sweet vanilla scent she wore. The softness of her skin against his. The warmth in those stunning blue eyes. And, oh, God, he wanted her. He really, really needed to feel her close to him.

Unable to help himself, he caught the tip of her finger between his lips.

Her eyes widened, and a hectic flush spread across her cheeks.

He ought to stop this. Right now.

And yet he found himself curling his fingers round her hand, moving it so her palm was against his lips, and pressing a kiss against her soft, soft skin. He folded her fingers over the place where he'd kissed her, still keeping his gaze locked with hers. And when her lips parted slightly, it was too much to resist. He leaned forward and brushed his mouth lightly against hers.

His lips tingled even more, and he couldn't help doing it again. And again. Until her arms slid round his neck and she started kissing him back.

It was only the sound of a car horn that shocked him back into common sense. And Marc was horrified when he realised that he was lying flat on the sofa, Laurie was sprawled over him, and he'd untucked her shirt and was stroking the bare skin on her back.

He closed his eyes. 'Laurie. I'm so sorry. I…' Oh, help. He didn't have a clue what to say.

'Me, too.' She wriggled off him, and restored order to her clothes.

'I shouldn't have done that.' His head and his common sense were firmly back in control, though his body was urging him not to listen to them and just yank her back into his arms.

'It was both of us,' she said.

Which was more generous than he deserved.

He dragged a hand through his hair. 'I hope this isn't going to make things awkward between us at work.'

Colour stained her cheeks. 'Because I jumped you, you mean?'

'That's not fair. I started the kissing business.'

'I touched you first,' she pointed out.

'OK. I guess we're both feeling guilty and embarrassed about this.'

She nodded.

'And we're both going to behave sensibly in future,' he said.

'Absolutely.' But then she reached forward to pick up her mug at the same time as he did, and their fingers touched. The tingle spread right through his body; and he could see it was the same for her, because her pupils went absolutely huge.

'Or,' she said softly, 'we could…admit something.'

All the air went out of his lungs.

Was she saying that she was attracted to him?

Well, Laurie Grant might be a fixer, and he'd noticed that she hugged people and was warm with everyone, but he didn't think she went around kissing people like this.

'You and me?' he asked, the words a hoarse whisper.

She lifted her chin. 'Just so you know, I don't make a habit of this sort of thing.'

He cupped her cheek with his palm. 'You didn't have to tell me. I know that's not you. Me neither.' She was the first since Ginny. The first woman he'd kissed like this, other than his wife, in more than ten years. Which made him feel incredibly guilty. This was wrong, wrong, wrong.

She turned her face to press a kiss into his palm, then gently removed his hand from her cheek and folded his fingers over the kiss, the same way that he'd done to her. 'So what are we going to do about this, Marc?'

What his body was urging him to do was to scoop her up and carry her upstairs to his bed.

His common sense was still in charge. Just.

'Neither of us needs any extra complications in our lives.'

'Absolutely,' she agreed.

'This—this *thing* between us would be a complication.'

'Indeed.'

Just as his common sense was doing a mental high-five and a victory dance, his libido fought back. 'But I want to.'

She moistened her lower lip. 'Me, too.'

The action undid him, and he leaned forward to kiss her on the mouth. It was meant to be a sweet, gentle, exploring kind of thing, but desire flared between them and the kiss turned much deeper and much, much hotter than he'd intended. By the time he broke the kiss her mouth was really reddened—and he was pretty sure his was in the same state.

'OK. So we've established that I like you and you like me,' he said. Because she deserved nothing less than honesty.

'Yes. And this is just between us. Nobody else needs to know about it.' She was still staring at his mouth, and it took all his strength not to wrap her back in his arms and kiss her until they were both dizzy.

'I thought you said everyone knew everything in a small town.'

'Not straight away. And we can be colleagues at work. Professional. Discreet.'

He stole another kiss. Making it quick, because he dared not linger. 'I'm not thinking discreet right now. I want to carry you to my bed.'

'Yes.' Her voice was husky, sexy as hell, and he very nearly did just what he'd just suggested.

But his common sense had some more ammunition. 'I feel guilty about this.'

'So do I. My mum's babysitting my little girl because I was doing a work thing this evening. I ought to be getting home and taking over from her.' She blew out a breath. 'But all I can think about right now is ripping your clothes off.'

Oh, yes. That worked for him. 'Laurie. My control's hanging by the thinnest of threads,' he warned. 'But we have to be sensible. I don't have a condom.'

'Me neither.' She gave him a rueful smile. 'Which makes things a little bit tricky for us.'

'There are other things we could...' He stopped

himself. 'Laurie. No. Go home. Now. Please. Before we both start behaving as if we're teenagers.'

She laughed. 'I think we already did that.' She indicated his sofa.

And how. The question burst out of him because right now he really, really needed to know. 'When could your mum babysit for you again?'

'Next Wednesday night, when we drop in to the village hall to see how the first exercise taster session is going.'

He swallowed hard. 'And we'd need to talk about it afterwards. Work together on a report. And here would be…quieter. More private.'

She shivered. 'I feel like a teenage girl planning prom night. Planning to…' She shook her head and closed her eyes for a moment. 'This is going to be a disaster.'

She'd changed her mind? Disappointment closed round his heart like a mailed fist. 'You're right. We should be sensible,' he said. 'Stick to being just colleagues.'

'I didn't mean that. I mean, it's been a while, for both of us. We're planning things. Expecting things. And I…' She paused and looked him straight in the eye. 'I don't want to disappoint you.'

It was the first time Marc had seen Laurie anything other than completely confident, and it shocked him.

But then he remembered that her ex had cheated on her. Including when she'd been giving birth to their daughter. That would've shattered anybody's confidence. And he guessed that Laurie was the type who'd smile to cover up her real feelings and pretend everything was just fine, even when it wasn't. Hadn't she said that you could always make the best of things? So her Pollyanna outlook was probably to stop herself getting hurt.

'You won't disappoint me,' he said softly. 'I like you, Laurie Grant. And that's a very good start.'

'Mmm-hmm.'

He took her hand and pressed it to the left side of his chest. 'There's your proof.'

Her eyes widened as she felt his heart thudding. 'Sorry. I'm being wet.'

'No apologies.' He stole the swiftest of kisses.

'No regrets. And no expectations. We'll see where this takes us, get to know each other.'

'Take it slowly,' she said.

Apart from the plans they'd made for next Wednesday night. Though he wasn't sure whether that thrilled him or scared him most. 'Yes.'

She nodded. 'I'll see you tomorrow at work, then.'

'OK.'

When he'd seen her out, he made himself another cup of coffee and sat down at the kitchen table.

He really hadn't expected this. A second chance. One that, despite what Laurie had said earlier, he still felt he didn't deserve.

He thought of Ginny.

'I don't love you any less,' he said softly. 'I'll miss you for the rest of my life. And I'll never forgive myself for letting you down. But I'm lonely, Gin. Bone-deep lonely. I think Laurie is, too. We're both on our own. And maybe we'll be able to help each other. Make things better for each other. Make some sense out of—well, all the things that have gone wrong for both of us.'

He smiled wryly. No expectations, they'd said. Yeah, right.

CHAPTER SEVEN

THE following Wednesday couldn't come quickly enough for either of them. Although they managed to keep their relationship completely professional at the surgery, Marc was very aware of Laurie. He knew the second she walked into a room, even if his back was to the door. Every time he looked at her, he felt as if he was burning up.

And tonight, he thought—tonight they'd have the ultimate closeness. He couldn't wait to hold her. Touch her.

But halfway through the Wednesday morning, Laurie had a call from the school secretary, Renee.

'Izzy's not feeling very well,' Renee explained. 'She says she's got a tummyache. I felt her forehead and she's definitely got a temperature.'

'Oh, no—poor baby. She was fine this morning. I wouldn't have sent her in otherwise,' Laurie said.

'It's not your fault. There's a bug doing the rounds. Can you come and pick her up?'

'I'll call my mum. If she can't come now, I'll talk to Leigh and see if the others can take on my patients. Tell Izzy I love her and she'll be home soon—and I'll ring you as soon as I know what's going on.'

To Laurie's relief, her mother was only pottering in the garden and was able to go and collect Izzy and look after her until Laurie had finished her shift. She quickly rang Renee back to explain that Diane was on her way.

At her break, she caught up with Marc. 'Izzy has a temperature and a tummyache. Mum's picked her up for me so I can finish my shift this morning, but I'm sorry, I'm going to have to ask you to do the project class on your own tonight. I'm not going to be able to make it.' And she really, really hoped that he could read between the lines of what she was saying.

'No worries.'

'It's not an excuse,' she said softly as they both left the staffroom. 'I'm not backing out of seeing you.'

'I know,' he said, keeping his voice low. 'But

you come as a package. Izzy needs to come first, and I accept that.'

'Thank you for being so understanding.'

He raised his voice back to normal tones. 'I'll collect the monitors from our patients. And it's the circuit training session, so it might be good for me to join in and do a class anyway.'

'OK.'

He lowered his voice again. 'And we'll take a rain-check on our other plans—until next Wednesday.'

Laurie's pulse spiked, and she went hot all over. 'Indeed.' And she flushed, knowing just how husky her voice sounded. And why. And because he knew why, too.

Part of her was aware how crazy this was. They didn't know each other that well. Neither of them was in the right place for a relationship— Marc was still grieving and blaming himself for his wife's death, and she was trying to keep life on an even keel for her little girl, which meant keeping any relationship under wraps until she was absolutely sure where it was going. Laurie didn't want to introduce a new man into Izzy's life until she was sure that it was what they all wanted.

And what she and Marc were planning to do...

Well, it wasn't a relationship, exactly. It was mutual attraction. And part of her really wanted to act on that attraction, to let her hair down for once and just enjoy it. Yet part of her worried that it was all going to go badly wrong. Had it been more than just an inability to take responsibility that had cracked her relationship with Dean? Or had that been his way of letting her down gently, and avoid having to tell her that she wasn't enough for him? If she let herself get close to Marc, would it go wrong?

She pushed the insecurities away. No. She had to look on the bright side, the way she always did. She liked Marc and Marc liked her. They were keeping this quiet to take the pressure off, for both of them. And they were just going to keep it light. Put a bit of fun and brightness into their lives. What was wrong with that?

Izzy still had a tummy ache when Laurie got home, but Laurie's mother had given the little girl a dose of infant paracetamol and put a cool cloth on her forehead, so her temperature was down, and the little girl was fast asleep.

'I read her a few stories from the princess book until she nodded off,' Diane said. 'Renee told me there's a bug going around. There were four other little ones waiting to be picked up when I got there.'

'Poor little mites. It's miserable feeling like this, especially when it's sunny outside and they'd rather be out in the playground with their friends. Thanks for rescuing me, Mum.'

'Any time.' Diane hugged Laurie. 'You know I'd be happy to do more to help you. If you weren't so independent...'

Laurie smiled. 'I know, Mum, and I appreciate it. But I don't want to take you for granted.' She grinned. 'No pun intended, Mrs Grant.'

'As if. You're worse than your father,' Diane teased.

'Have you had any lunch yet?' Laurie asked.

'I waited for you. I made us a salad,' Diane said. 'And I had some cold salmon in the fridge from last night, so I brought that over with me.'

'Mum, that's wonderful. Thank you. And you spoil me.'

'That's what mums are for. No doubt you'll do the same for Izzy.' She paused. 'And for her brothers and sisters.'

Laurie shook her head. 'That's not going to happen, Mum.'

'Because you never do anything where you actually meet people, other than the mums of other children at school,' Diane said.

Laurie smiled. 'I'm hardly going clubbing at my age.'

'Anyone would think you were fifty, not thirty!' Diane rolled her eyes. 'I just wish you'd take some time for yourself and—well, I know Dean hurt you, but not all men are like that.'

'I know. You'll be ganging up with Fiona next,' Laurie said lightly. 'She wants me to be as happily settled as she is. But I'm fine as I am. Really.'

'Hmm. An only child's a lonely child.'

'No, she's not. Izzy has plenty of friends, plus she has me and you and Dad—not to mention her Uncle Joe, Aunty Rose and her cousins. It's fine, Mum.' Laurie smiled to take the sting from her words. 'Let's have some lunch.'

* * *

Marc wasn't surprised when Laurie wasn't at work, the next morning. He'd already seen a couple of children from Izzy's school, the previous day, and the tummy bug seemed to be lasting for about three days. It was unlikely that Laurie would be back until Monday.

Leigh, the practice manager, had arranged a locum to cover Laurie's shifts—thankfully not the one who'd upset so many patients before—and Marc grabbed a moment during his morning break to call Laurie.

'How's Izzy doing?'

'Still feeling rough, poor love. I'm giving her lots of sips of cool water, and hopefully she'll be able to manage something at lunchtime.'

'How are *you* doing,' he asked softly.

'I'm OK. You?'

He took a risk. 'I missed you last night.'

'Me, too.'

Funny how that quiet little admission sent a thrill all the way through him.

'How was the class?' she asked.

'Surprisingly fun. I think our patients enjoyed it, too.' He paused. 'I collected all the monitors. Do you want me to drop them off to your friend Jay?'

'No, it's OK. I was going to drop them at his place rather than his office—it's a good excuse to see Fiona and the baby. If Izzy's up to it, I was planning to do that on Saturday after we've fed the ducks. And I should be back at work on Monday.' He noticed that she didn't ask him to feed the ducks with her this week. She'd admitted that she'd missed him, but was she also having second thoughts about what they were planning, confused about whether they were doing the right thing? He was, too. And yet she still drew him.

Izzy was much better on Saturday, so Laurie rang her best friend. 'Fiona, I need to get these monitors back to Jay. Izzy's been off for the last couple of days with a bug; she's OK now, but I can just drop them off and not come in, if you like, to make sure the baby doesn't pick up any germs.'

'Don't be daft,' Fiona said. 'It'll be lovely to see you both. What time can you come over?'

'After we've fed the ducks? I promised Iz some fresh air.'

'Great. You can stay for lunch. Jay's out playing squash, so we can have a girly chat and Iz can draw me one of her fabulous pictures.'

After she'd taken Izzy to feed the ducks, Laurie picked up some sweet-scented stocks from the florist in the middle of town, then drove over to Fiona's with the monitors she'd borrowed from Jay.

Fiona greeted her with a hug, and made them both coffee after she'd seated Izzy at the table with a glass of milk, paper and crayons. 'I hear the new doctor in your practice is very dishy,' she said.

'He's a nice guy,' Laurie said carefully. 'He fits in well in the practice, and he's helping me with my pet project.'

Fiona raised an eyebrow. 'Is he single?'

'Mum's already given me a lecture this week about dating, and that's more than enough. Don't you start, too,' Laurie said with a groan.

'Your mum has a point,' Fiona said. 'It might be good for you to meet someone. You're a great mum to Izzy, but you need some time for you as well.'

'I'm fine.' But Laurie could feel the betraying heat in her face.

Fiona looked interested. 'You're blushing, Laurie. Anything you want to tell me?'

'No.' Even though Fiona was her best friend and Izzy's godmother, Laurie didn't want to say a word to her until she was sure where this thing with Marc was going.

Fiona smiled. 'Jay said he was a nice guy.'

'Jay,' Laurie said, blowing out a breath, 'is stirring.'

Fiona gave her a hug. 'Sorry, I know I shouldn't tease you—but it'd be so nice to see you having some fun in your life.'

'I do have fun.'

'I know you do, with Izzy, but you know what I meant—you deserve someone who's going to treat you better than That Man did.'

Laurie shrugged. 'I'm doing OK. Really. Now, is Eve asleep or do I get the cuddle I've been looking forward to all week?'

To her relief, Fiona allowed herself to be distracted by the baby and dropped the subject.

* * *

On the Wednesday evening, Diane was looking after Izzy, as arranged, and Laurie went to the kick-boxing taster session at the village hall. She arrived early, in case anyone had questions for her, and she was pleased to see that everyone in the group turned up to give it a try.

'I don't think it's for me—I'm never going to be like that Jackie Chan,' Russell Parker confided, 'but my son said I ought to come along and give it a go, and it might not be as bad as I think it is.'

'And he's absolutely right,' Laurie said with a smile.

Several other patients came over to chat to her and say how much they were enjoying the taster sessions—and that they'd been surprised by the sheer range of exercise available. Some had even talked their partners into being their exercise buddies, once they'd found something they wanted to do again.

Laurie was really glad that it was working out how she'd hoped it would, but at the same time she was desperate for the class to be over. After this, she'd arranged to call in to see Marc to discuss how the session had gone, and then…

She felt hot all over. She'd actually arranged to meet him in the full knowledge that they would be going to bed together, and it made her feel scared and excited all at the same time. Did he feel as mixed up as this, she wondered, wanting so desperately to do it and yet worrying that it was all going to go wrong?

After the session, everyone helped clear up. Several of the patients sounded enthusiastic about doing a beginners' martial arts class in the future, and the class leader took their names with a smile.

Finally, the village hall janitor arrived and locked up. And then Laurie drove to Marc's house. She parked outside and just sat there for a moment, her pulse hammering. What if he'd changed his mind? Was she about to make an enormous fool of herself?

Her mobile phone rang and she jumped. She grabbed it from her handbag, just in case it was her mother and there was a problem with Izzy, but Marc's name was on the screen.

She answered the call warily. 'Hello?'

'Are you going to sit there in your car all night, Laurie, or do you want to come in?' He sounded amused, but she could hear the tension in his voice, too. So he was as worried about this as she was. Thinking about what could go wrong. How awkward it could become at work.

And, paradoxically, that made her feel better. 'I'm on my way,' she mumbled.

He opened the front door to her. 'So how did the session go?'

'It was good fun. I did a few of the moves with them, and I might be tempted to go along to the beginners' class myself. Everyone turned up again, so we must be doing something right.' She grimaced. 'Sorry, I'm talking too much. I'll shut up now.'

He closed the door behind her and smiled. 'Does it help if I tell you that I'm nervous, too?'

'Yes.' She swallowed hard. 'So it's…' Her throat dried. 'It's still on?' she finished.

'Unless you want to call a halt.'

'I haven't been able to stop thinking about this all day,' she admitted huskily.

'Good, because neither have I—and I've been

on a slow burn all week, remembering what it feels like to kiss you.'

His eyes were very dark, and his words melted her. She said nothing, just tipped her head back. He gave her a slow, sweet smile, and then wrapped his arms round her. And it felt like heaven. He brushed his mouth against hers, teasing and enticing and demanding all at the same time; she slid her fingers into his hair and kissed him back.

When he broke the kiss, they were both shaking. Laurie couldn't remember the last time she'd felt this burning need.

Marc took the scrunchie from her hair and let her hair fall around her shoulders. 'Your hair's amazing.' He twined a curl round his finger. 'Soft, like silk.' His voice deepened. 'And I'm dying to know what your skin feels like.'

'Me, too. Yours, I mean, not mine.' Her words sounded croaky, but he didn't laugh at her; he just gave her an intense, smouldering look, took her hand and led her upstairs.

He paused at a doorway. 'Give me two seconds.'

Laurie could hardly breathe, knowing that she

was going to walk through that door into his bedroom, take her clothes off, and make love with him.

They barely knew each other. She was going to have sex with a near-stranger. This was totally shocking. Totally un-Laurie-like behaviour.

Yet, at the same time, they'd spent enough time together to know what damage the other had been through. She knew they'd be careful with each other. This would be *safe*.

So why did it feel so dangerous?

Marc reappeared in the doorway. 'Just so you know, I rented this house furnished. And I bought all new linen and soft furnishings when I moved.'

She knew exactly what he was telling her. The bed they were about to share he hadn't shared with anyone else. There were no memories for him, and she didn't need to worry that he was going to compare her to anyone. And she really appreciated that reassurance. 'Thank you.'

He rubbed the pad of his thumb gently along her lower lip. 'You're very welcome.'

He led her into his room. It was quaintly old-fashioned with a four-poster bed, a polished wooden floor and a fireplace that clearly wasn't used because the place for the firebox was filled with dried flowers. He'd lit scented tea-light candles on the mantelpiece, and the soft light made the room incredibly romantic. And at last Laurie stopped feeling faintly cheap and grubby.

'So, Dr Grant.' Marc leaned forward and stole a kiss. 'What now?'

He was wearing a formal shirt, but without a tie and with the top button undone. Not saying a word, Laurie reached up and undid all the rest of the buttons, before untucking the soft cotton from his waistband and pushing his shirt off his shoulders.

His eyes glittered. 'What a good idea.' He did the same with her shirt; Laurie could hardly breathe as he undid the buttons and his fingers brushed against her skin.

Slowly, wordlessly, they undressed each other down to their underwear.

She felt ridiculously shy, like a teenager all over again.

As if he understood, he whispered, 'Close your eyes.'

She did so, and felt him unclip her bra. And then he scooped her up.

Laurie opened her eyes again. 'Marc, what about your arm?'

'It healed a long time ago. And lifting you onto my bed isn't going to do any damage,' he reassured her. 'It's not as if you're a rugby prop forward who's built like a brick outhouse and I'm just about to collide with you at speed.'

She relaxed and let him lift her onto the bed.

There were cool, smooth cotton sheets against her back, and her head rested on the softest of down pillows. She felt the mattress dip slightly as he climbed onto the bed beside her. She was glad he'd opted for the softer lighting when she realised that he'd already removed his underpants and was curling his fingers round the elastic of her knickers. She lifted herself from the bed so he could peel them down

She wanted this so badly, yet at the same time it made her panic. She could still remember the mechanics of what they were about to do, but she hadn't remembered the feelings; that sudden rush of desire was overwhelming.

He kissed her lightly. 'If you're having second thoughts, that's fine. We'll stop.'

'It's just... Well, it's been a while,' she said, 'and it feels like the first time all over again.'

He smiled at her. 'Technically, it *is* the first time. For us. If it makes you feel any better, I'm terrified that I'm going to be rubbish—I don't know where and how you like being touched, what pleases you, anything.'

'Same here.' She bit her lip. 'Maybe we should just be brave and explore together?'

'That,' he said, 'is a brilliant idea.' He dipped his head to kiss her, then shifted so he could kiss his way down the side of her neck.

'That's nice,' she whispered.

Emboldened by the way he was touching her, she began to explore him, stroking his back. She knew she'd found a place he liked when he arched against her and sighed with pleasure.

He kissed the hollows of her collarbones, then along her sternum, and she arched up to him. He cupped her breasts, took one nipple into his mouth and sucked. Laurie felt herself grow wet with desire, and rocked against him slightly. 'More,' she whispered.

Marc toyed with her other nipple, then finally slid one hand between her thighs. He stroked and teased until she was close to whimpering. She pushed herself against his hand, and then finally he eased one finger into her; she gave a sigh of relief.

'Better?' he asked.

She nodded. 'Sorry.'

'No apologies,' he reminded her. 'I'm exploring and finding out what you like.' He circled his thumb on her clitoris as he continued pushing inside her.

Laurie was shocked by the speed of her orgasm; within only a few seconds she fell apart in his arms.

'I wanted that first time to be for you,' he said softly, 'and now I think you're ready.'

She heard the rip of a foil packet, the snap as he rolled the condom on. And then, oh, bliss, he was kneeling between her thighs, fitting himself to her entrance and slowly, slowly easing into her. She reached up to jam her mouth over his, mimicking with her tongue what he was doing to her with his body.

Unbelievably, she felt her body tightening all

over again. This was crazy. She shouldn't feel so in tune with him Shouldn't the first time be messy and awkward and a bit embarrassing?

And then she stopped thinking as she climaxed again, and felt his body surge in answer against hers.

He held her close until both their heart rates had slowed back to normal, then gently eased out of her. 'I'd better deal with the condom.'

When he came back from the bathroom, she'd pulled the sheet over herself, feeling shy. He was still completely naked. He stopped short as he saw her, his eyes widening.

'You're beautiful,' she said.

'So are you. Under that sheet.' He joined her underneath it, and held her close with her head pillowed on his shoulder. 'Thank you.'

'Thank you.' She shifted so she could press a kiss against his chest. 'That was pretty amazing.'

'So what now?' he asked.

'No expectations, we said.'

'And no regrets.' He drew her closer. 'I liked being a teenager all over again.'

'So you're saying you want to do this all over again?'

He shifted so that he could look her straight in the eye. 'Do you?'

'I asked first.'

He stroked her cheek. 'Yes. I know it's complicated, I know you come as part of a package, and I know I'm an emotional mess. But I still want to do this again. With you.' He paused. 'And you?'

She nodded. 'But I'm not ready to go public, Marc. Not for a while.'

'Uh-huh.'

'Not because I don't like you—I do, or I wouldn't be here, because I don't go off and have hot monkey sex with just *anybody*—but I have Izzy to think about.'

'Of course you do.' He kissed her lightly. 'Speaking of her, you need to get back before your mum starts worrying about you.'

'I did tell her that I was going to see you before I came home, talk about the project with you.'

'And you did.' He grinned. 'Just not for very long.'

'I guess we both got a little bit distracted.'

'Hot monkey sex. Hmm.' He stole another

kiss. 'So is this going to be same time, same place, next week?'

'It's your turn to do the class next week,' she pointed out. 'And I can't offer you anything more than coffee afterwards.'

'OK. Just coffee. I'll take the offer.' The corners of his eyes crinkled. 'Even if it is instant stuff out of a jar.'

'You're such a coffee snob,' she teased back.

He kissed her lightly. 'I'll get you a fresh towel so you can have a shower. And, much as I'd like to, I'm not going to join you. Otherwise you'll have to explain to your mother why your hair's wet. And I'm not sure how she'd react to the idea of you having hot monkey sex in a shower.'

She couldn't help smiling. 'You like that phrase, don't you?'

'You're the one who used it first,' he reminded her, and stole another kiss. 'See you downstairs. I'll leave a fresh towel outside the door.'

'Thanks.'

It felt strange, showering in someone else's bathroom, and Laurie got herself ready in double-quick time. Her clothes were slightly rumpled, but hopefully her mother wouldn't notice.

Marc gave her a lingering kiss goodbye. 'See you at work in the morning, Dr Grant. And if you're good I might even buy you a sweet chilli chicken salad wrap from the patisserie and feed the ducks with you at lunchtime.'

'That,' Laurie said with a grin, 'is a date.'

CHAPTER EIGHT

MARC and Laurie headed for the patisserie on Thursday lunchtime to buy sandwiches—running the gauntlet of more good-natured teasing by Tina—and ate them in the sunshine on the bench by the duck pond.

There was nobody around to hear him, but Marc lowered his voice anyway. 'Right now, Dr Grant, I'd really like to kiss you. Like I did last night.'

Laurie went deliciously pink. And then he remembered how she'd looked as she'd climaxed, her eyes wide and her skin flushed like that, and went decidedly hot under his own collar.

'Marc,' she said in a warning whisper.

'I'm not going to do it—at least, not in the middle of the town where anyone could see us and start gossiping,' he reassured her. 'Besides, we don't want to scare the ducks.'

To his relief, she smiled back. 'Absolutely. Otherwise I'll have to give them double rations next time I come.'

'Saturday morning?' he asked.

'Not this week—I checked the weather forecast and it's going to be glorious, so I'm taking Izzy to the beach.' She gave him a sidelong look. 'How are you on rock pools and crabbing?'

'Rock pools and crabbing?' he echoed, mystified.

She shook her head and tutted. 'You're such a Londoner! I was wondering, would you like to come with us?' When he said nothing, she added softly, 'No strings.'

Well, he knew she came as a package. And he wanted to see more of her. So he'd just have to shove all the guilt back where it came from, and make an effort to get to know Izzy, too. 'I'd like that. Thank you.'

'Shall I pick you up at nine?' she suggested.

'Or I could pick you up.'

She shook her head. 'Izzy's seat is already in my car. Besides, I wouldn't want to get yours messy.'

'I'm not that much of a neat freak,' he said.

'No?' she teased.

'No.' He couldn't resist leaning closer and whispering, 'And you can ruffle me any time you like, Dr Grant.'

'Marc!' But she was laughing.

'What do I need to bring?'

'Nothing—I have the bucket, spade, beach towels and sun cream. So just yourself.'

'Is Cocoa coming, too?'

'Dogs aren't allowed on the beach in summer, so Mum and Dad are going to pop round to let him out. It'll be just the three of us.'

Just the three of us.

He was being given a second chance at a family.

Did he dare to take it?

On Saturday morning, Laurie knocked on Marc's front door at nine. She was wearing cut-off faded denim shorts, a bright pink T-shirt and espadrilles, and looked adorably cute. He itched to kiss her but he knew that he couldn't, not with Izzy there. Before they went public, she'd need to talk to Izzy. And, given how Laurie's relationship with Dean had ended and the way the man had destroyed her trust, Marc knew that it would take a while until she was ready. Giving her time to get used to the idea worked for him, too; he wasn't entirely sure that he was ready for this. Though he did know that he wanted to see more of Laurie.

The little girl greeted him with delight when he got into the car. 'Hello, Marc. Mummy says you're coming crabbing with us.'

'Yes.' He made an effort. 'I've never done it before.'

She smiled shyly at him. 'I have. Three whole times.'

'So can you teach me how to do it?'

She looked thrilled at the idea. 'You bet I can!'

This time, he felt much more at ease with her, less panicky than he'd been the day they'd gone to the bluebell woods, and he even found himself joining in with the songs that Izzy and Laurie sang in the car, with a bit of prompting from Izzy.

Laurie parked on the cliffs at the edge of the town. 'I thought it'd be nice to walk down the cliff path to the seafront,' she said.

Marc fell in love with the old Victorian seaside resort, with its promenade and its pier with the lifeboat house on the end. 'This really isn't what I expected,' he said. 'I thought Norfolk was all really huge flat beaches?'

'You're thinking of Wells and Holkham, the ones that tend to be used as film sets,' she said. 'We have cliffs too, here at Cromer and then the stripy ones out at Hunstanton. They found a mammoth in the cliffs just up the road a few years ago.'

He looked at her, intrigued. 'So does that mean we can go fossil hunting?'

'This particular beach isn't quite in the same league as Lyme Regis or Whitby when it comes to fossils,' she said with a smile, 'but we can look. And even if we don't find an actual fossil, there are lots of pretty pebbles.' She ruffled Izzy's hair. 'The tide's in, so shall we go crabbing first?'

She led them onto the pier, where they hired a line and bucket and bought some bait. Izzy showed him how to wind out the string, and how to wind it up again. It took them half an hour to catch a single tiny crab, but Izzy was delighted.

'And now we have to put it back, so it can grow big and its mum doesn't worry about it,' she said.

When they'd returned their crabbing equipment, they stopped to buy ice creams. Marc was quietly amused to notice that the little girl liked sprinkles on her ice cream as well as a chocolate flake, and he let her choose the topping for his own cone. How many years had it been since he'd last eaten one of those? he wondered as he tasted the sweet, creamy mixture. How many years since he'd felt as carefree as this, with the sound of the waves lapping at the shore, the tangy scent of the sea in his nostrils, huge white gulls shrieking above, the sun warming him and white streaky clouds scudding across a deep blue sky?

By the time they'd finished their ice creams, the tide had gone out enough to leave shallow pools around the rocks. Several families were already there, peering into the clear water and pointing things out to each other.

'Can we go 'sploring, Mummy?' Izzy asked.

'Of course we can, darling. But remember what Granddad said about not having bare feet on the rocks?'

'In case you get cuts on your feet,' Izzy said solemnly.

Laurie rummaged in her beach bag and retrieved some flip-flops. Izzy took her trainers off and changed into the flip-flops; Laurie tucked her shoes and Izzy's back into the bag.

Marc removed his trainers and rolled his jeans up above his calves before following them onto the beach. The wet sand felt beautifully cool against his feet. He was amused to notice that Laurie's toenails were painted a very bright pink; he hadn't noticed that on Wednesday when she'd been in his bed, but then again he hadn't exactly been looking at her feet. He'd needed to touch her and taste her and lose himself in her.

He thoroughly enjoyed poking around the rock pools with Izzy. They found more tiny crabs, and the highlight for the little girl was when they found a sea anemone and a starfish. Laurie was watching them both, and Marc shared a complicit smile with her; the little girl's delight was infectious.

When Izzy had had enough of the rock pools, Marc helped her to make a big sandcastle with a moat. They decorated the towers at the corners with seaweed, and then Marc took her to the water's edge to fill her bucket with water so she could tip it into the moat. The sea was cool but delicious against his skin.

Izzy tipped the water from her bucket into the moat; it drained away quickly, but stayed for just long enough for Laurie to take a picture of Marc and Izzy together with their moated castle.

Marc couldn't remember the last time he'd felt this relaxed or had had such fun. Was this what it would've been like with his own child? He pushed the thought away. Now wasn't the time or the place.

They ate fish and chips sitting on one of the benches on the seafront; a line of gulls perched on a nearby wall watching them with beady eyes and waiting for one of them to drop a chip or some fish so they could swoop on it.

'This is fabulous,' Marc said.

'Didn't you live near a seaside where you lived before?' Izzy asked.

'I lived in London so, no, there isn't a beach. There used to be a little one by the Tower of London, but that was a lot of years ago, when my granddad was tiny.'

'So that's why you never went crabbing before?' she asked.

'That's right. But I really enjoyed today, and I hope we can do this again later in the summer.'

Izzy glanced at her mother, waiting for her nod before saying, 'Yes, please!'

As they walked back up the cliff path to the car park, Marc noticed that the little girl's steps were flagging. She was clearly tired, He could leave it to Laurie to deal with the situation. Or he could make an effort—the way Laurie had when she'd invited him to share her day. He could do what any other man would do in this situation when a friend's child was tired and his friend had her hands full. Even though it felt scarily like taking things another step forward.

'Would it be OK for me to give her a piggyback?' he asked Laurie quietly.

Laurie looked concerned. 'What about your shoulder?'

'My shoulder's fine—really—and Izzy's not exactly heavy. I can carry her.'

'If you're sure, thanks.' Laurie gave him a grateful smile.

'Izzy, are your legs tired?' he asked.

At her reluctant nod, he said, 'How about a piggyback?'

'Like the ones Granddad gives me?' At his nod, she beamed. 'Oh, yes, please!'

It warmed him that Laurie trusted him with her most precious possession, and Marc was careful to make sure that Izzy was comfortable and that he was holding her securely as he gave her a piggyback up the cliff path.

'That was brilliant. Thank you,' Izzy said as they got to the car and he set her down.

She fell asleep in the car on the way home, and Marc couldn't help feeling antsy on the way back. Today had been a revelation. A joy. Yet, at the same time, it scared him witless how easy it was to get close to Laurie and Izzy.

Too close.

He hadn't expected it to be like this, and he wanted it to stay like this and he wanted to back away in equal measures. Laurie had said that her parents were going to drop round to let Cocoa out. Would they still be there? Had Laurie said anything to them about him? He really wasn't ready to make their relationship public.

But when they got back to the village Marc was relieved to note that there was no car parked outside Laurie's house. So meeting her parents was something he didn't have to face just yet.

'Do you want me to carry her in?' he asked when Laurie parked the car.

'Thanks, that'd be good. We've tired her out.' She smiled. 'I think I'm just going to put her to bed as she is. She can have a soak in the bath tomorrow to get the sand out.'

He carried Izzy upstairs, following Laurie into the smaller bedroom. He wasn't in the slightest bit surprised that Izzy's bedroom was full of pink and purple and sparkly things. Laurie pulled the duvet back and he laid the little girl down gently on the bed. Izzy stayed fast asleep while Laurie gently removed her flip-flops and drew the duvet over her. And the look of sheer love on her face as she kissed the little girl's cheek made Marc's stomach clench. Loving someone like that was dangerous. It meant you had everything to lose. And he'd learned that the hard way. Losing everything wasn't something he'd risk. Ever again.

'Do you want to stay for a coffee?' she asked when they went downstairs.

'That'd be lovely.' He could put up with her

awful coffee for the sake of spending more time with her.

'Go and sit down. Put some music on, if you like.'

He didn't, though he did look through her CDs and found out that she liked pop music rather than the mixture of classic rock and classical music that he favoured.

When she brought the mugs in, he was surprised to discover that she was actually giving him proper coffee, with a layer of *crema* on top. Then again, he knew that some brands of instant coffee mimicked the effect. He sniffed the brew experimentally and smiled. This was definitely proper coffee. And he realised that she'd done this especially for him.

'Did you go out and buy a coffee machine?' he asked.

'Nothing like as fancy or as expensive as yours,' she said. 'It's just one of those French presses—the one where you push a plunger down in a glass jug.'

'It does the job.' He tasted it. 'And that's a very nice coffee blend, Dr Grant.'

'It's Italian roast—though I'm afraid it's from

the supermarket, not the kind of posh deli a coffee purist like you would get yours from,' she teased.

'I'm not that much of a purist. And this is a million times nicer than the last coffee you made me. Thank you.'

He noticed the dimple in her cheek when she smiled. It was the same as the dimple in Izzy's cheek when she'd seen the starfish.

Funny, a month ago he would've run a mile from this. He still wasn't entirely comfortable with the situation, still felt those prickles of guilt, but there was also a warmth and a lightness in his soul that he'd never expected to feel again. 'Thank you for asking me to go with you today. I enjoyed every second of it.'

'Me, too,' she said softly, and her cheeks went adorably pink.

'Laurie, I know that, here and now, I can't do with you what I really want to do—it's not appropriate, with Izzy asleep upstairs—but can I at least hold you?'

She nodded, put her coffee down and went over to join him. Marc scooped her onto his lap and held her close. Funny, just being with her made him feel better.

The dog had clearly decided that he wasn't going to be left out, and sneaked up onto the sofa next to them.

Laurie looked at the dog and sighed. 'Cocoa, you know you're not supposed to be there.'

The Labrador gave her a guilty wag of his tail, and looked up at her with big, pleading brown eyes.

'Oh, you impossible dog! All right, I neglected you today, so you can stay put. As long as Marc doesn't mind you huffing all over him.'

'I like dogs.' He scratched the top of the Labrador's head. Weird how this felt so much like being at home. The centre of a family. Everything he'd always wanted—everything he'd cut himself off from because he knew he didn't deserve it.

'I'm probably not as strict with him as I should be,' Laurie admitted.

'Would I be right in guessing he's a rescue dog?' Marc asked.

'Well—yes. He was six months old when he came to live with us. Everyone said I shouldn't take him in, because Iz was a toddler and you never know how dogs are going to react, but all he needed was some love. He adores Iz, and he's the gentlest dog I've ever met. Completely daft, but gentle.'

All he needed was some love. Dr Fixit had seen that straight away, and the dog had clearly responded in kind.

She wrinkled her nose. 'I suppose I do spoil him a bit, but how can you resist those gorgeous big brown eyes?'

Marc made his eyes as wide as possible and gave her a soulful look over the rim of his glasses, and she burst out laughing. 'It's not quite the same, Marc. Your eyes aren't brown. There's green and gold mixed in there, too.'

'I can do the eye thing. Cocoa will teach me— won't you, boy?'

The Labrador's tail thumped.

Marc kissed her lingeringly; then he was content just to sit with her, holding her close.

'I got some fabulous photos from today. I love that one of you and Iz with the sandcastle. I'll email it to you when I've transferred the pictures to my laptop.'

'That'd be nice.' He kissed the top of her head. 'I've never met anyone who takes quite so many photos.'

'I like photos.' She gestured to the line of frames on the mantelpiece.

Even though he hadn't met her family yet, the likeness in the portraits was obvious—her parents, her brother—and what struck him most was that every photograph was filled to the brim with what he'd been missing since the day Ginny died.

Love.

And he stuffed the thought immediately in the box in his head marked 'Do not open'.

Reluctantly, at the end of the evening Marc took his leave and kissed Laurie goodnight. 'I'll see you on Monday morning,' he said softly.

The next morning, he opened his email to discover the photographs from Laurie, and he was stunned. It was the first time he'd seen himself without shadows in his eyes since the day of Ginny's funeral. He actually looked happy.

He thought about it and realised that he *was* happy, and it was Laurie who'd taken the weight off his shoulders. She'd made him really think about the burden of guilt he'd been carrying. He knew it would never go completely, but it had lightened. Though he felt guilty about that, too

Maybe it was time he tackled some of the unpacking he'd been avoiding.

He replied swiftly to Laurie's email, thanking her for the photographs, then closed his laptop, headed to the dining room, slit the packing tape on the first box and opened it.

Over the rest of the day he worked his way steadily through the boxes. He put his books on the shelves in the living room, along with his music and films. So much of this had been shared with Ginny, but depriving himself of it wasn't going to bring her back or make him feel better. Maybe Laurie was right and it was time to remember the good stuff instead of looking at the might-have-beens.

But the one thing he couldn't quite bring himself to unpack was the box he knew was full of photographs. He needed to wait just a little longer before he could cope with that.

Wednesday it was Marc's turn to go along to the taster class; this time it was the ballroom dancing class, and although he enjoyed himself he wished that Laurie had been there with him. He would've liked to hold her, dance with her. And nobody would've speculated about them being together, because he and Laurie were both there for the sake of their patients.

He called in to see her afterwards, to update her on how the evening had gone.

'It's a shame you didn't come along. We learned how to do a social foxtrot.' He smiled. 'I danced with all the women in our group. It was great fun.'

'You're such a flirt, Dr Bailey,' she teased.

'The teacher was really nice. I think some of our patients are going to take it up—and apparently doing the cha-cha and the quickstep, if you do a whole hour's dancing, is nearly as good as doing a cardio class.'

'Except it doesn't feel like exercise—and if it's something they can do with a friend or their partner and it's good for their social lives as well as their fitness levels, so much the better,' she said.

They sat on the sofa with Laurie on Marc's lap and Cocoa curled up beside him.

'Do you fancy doing something together this weekend?' he asked.

'What were you thinking?'

'What sort of thing does Izzy like doing?'

'We could go to the park. She loves the swings and slides, and we could kick a ball around. Or the cinema, if you don't mind sitting through an animated movie—I should warn you now that she adores princesses, so it'll be a really girly animated movie.'

'I guess it depends on what's showing and what the weather's going to be like. And maybe we could go out for a meal afterwards.'

'That would be lovely. There's a nice American diner that Izzy likes—we sometimes go there with my parents.' She paused. 'My parents are planning to have a barbecue on Sunday. You could come with us.'

Meet her family. Admit that they were a couple. Marc wasn't quite sure he was ready for that. 'I'm sure your family is as charming as you are,' he said softly, 'but are you ready to be outed yet?'

'No,' she admitted, to his secret relief. 'I'm enjoying having you all to myself for the moment, and I'd rather wait a little longer and talk to Izzy about it first before we go public.' She stroked his face and there was a look of mischief in her expression when she said, 'But I do have another idea.'

'I'm all ears.'

'Izzy's going to Molly's after school on Monday. For tea. I don't have to pick her up until half six.'

He nuzzled her cheek. 'Which means you'd be free to come and have an early dinner with me.'

She looked surprised. 'You can cook?'

'How does it go? Let me think. Pasta, garlic bread, salad, nothing special…' He grinned.

She laughed back. 'That's my line. Actually, that sounds wonderful. I'd love to.'

CHAPTER NINE

ON SATURDAY afternoon, Izzy looked pleased to see Marc when he turned up at their house. 'Are you coming round to have a play date?' Izzy asked.

'Sort of. I thought maybe we could go out somewhere, like that day we had at the seaside. So I was wondering, would you like to go to the cinema or the park?' he asked.

'With Mummy, too?'

'With your mum, too,' he confirmed.

The little girl thought about it. 'The sun's all shiny and nice, so can we go to the park, please?'

'Sure. That sounds like fun.'

'And will you play ball with me?'

'Of course I will.'

Marc was surprised to discover how much he enjoyed their time in the park. Once they'd played piggy-in-the-middle and he'd taught Izzy how to dribble a ball, they went over to the play area. Marc pushed Izzy on the swings, making her shriek with joy as she went higher; he lifted her so she could swing on the monkey bars, but kept close enough so he could catch her if she lost her balance; and he timed her on the slide to see how fast she could go.

He'd just finished timing her third go on the slide when she said, 'Look, it's Georgia!' She beamed and ran over to her best friend, then hugged her tightly.

Tina came over to join them. 'Fancy seeing you both here. Together.' She looked meaningfully at Marc. 'I didn't know you had children, Dr Bailey.'

'I don't,' he admitted.

She raised an eyebrow. 'So you're here with Laurie and Izzy, then?'

Marc exchanged a glance with Laurie. Was she ready to tell her friend the truth about their burgeoning relationship, or would she want to keep it quiet and just between the two of them for a bit longer?

'We're being very boring and talking shop,' Laurie said. 'It's hard to find enough hours in the day. You know that Marc's helping me with my project—we're taking the chance to catch up with that.'

It wasn't a *total* fib, Marc thought with a throb of guilt. They probably would discuss it at some point during the day. And he felt even guiltier about being relieved that Laurie wasn't ready to go public yet.

'I'd heard about that—well, actually, Mum did, in the shop,' Tina said. 'She's been talking to Judy Reynolds, who says it's brilliant and Wednesdays are now her favourite day of the week.'

'I think we can safely say that's a result, Laurie,' Marc said with a grin, giving her a high five.

'Mum asked me if I could have a word with you about adding her to it,' Tina said. 'She says she's getting terrible middle-age spread and she's trying to eat sensibly—she never even tastes the stuff she makes at the shop—but she just hasn't got time to do an exercise class.' She grimaced. 'Well, she *says* she hasn't got time, but I think it's because she doesn't like it. She really hated that new dance class she did with me a couple of months ago. She said it was too fast and she couldn't follow most of the moves, and I guess she was right.' Tina sighed. 'I've tried asking her to come to the gym with me, but she won't—even though I told her there are plenty of other women there her age and she won't be out of place.'

'We had a ballroom dancing session last week,' Marc said, and 'I think there's going to be a beginners' class set up some time very soon, if she wants to try that.'

'I bet she'd love it, but talking Dad into being her partner and going with her...' Tina looked wistful. 'That's so not going to happen. She says she only just persuaded him to dance at their wedding, and she had to nag him like mad to dance at mine!'

'If she went on her own, there'd be someone there she could dance with,' Laurie said. 'Or there's aqua aerobics.'

'That's mainly resistance work,' Marc said, 'so it's not going to make her feel as wiped out as a more advanced dance class or doing high-impact aerobics, but it'll still give her a good workout and get her heart rate up safely. The water's a supportive environment, so it'll be kind to her joints, too.'

Tina looked thoughtful. 'I did aqua aerobics as an antenatal class and really enjoyed it. I'll suggest that to her.'

'Or tell her to come to the village hall on Wednesday at eight,' Laurie said. 'I'm not sure if I'll be able to get her on to the monitoring side of the project—that depends on whether or not my friend Jay still has some gaps—but there's no reason why your mum can't do the taster sessions with everyone else. I can email you the schedule so she can see if there's anything she fancies trying.'

'That'd be great. Thanks, Laurie.' Tina hugged her. 'Georgia, honey, we need to go—we've got to pick up some shopping for Nanna and Granddad. See you later, Laurie. Marc.' She smiled at them.

'That was a close call,' Marc said when Tina was out of earshot and Izzy was back on the slide. 'Do you think she'll say anything?'

Laurie shook her head. 'Tina knows I juggle things and multi-task like crazy—and that you're working on the project with me. And it wasn't a total fib about us talking shop.'

'No.' He paused. 'What if she did say something?'

'I hope she doesn't. I'd rather Izzy heard it from us,' Laurie said. 'Don't take this the wrong way, Marc, but it's still early stages. I'm not ashamed of what we're doing, but I'm also not ready for Izzy to think we're anything other than just friends.'

He really wasn't ready to go public. And if Laurie had been…everything would have started to unravel. He wasn't ready for that either.

'That's fine,' he said lightly. 'And you're absolutely right—it's still early stages. We're taking things slowly.'

When they'd finished at the park, they headed back to Laurie's to let Cocoa out and for Izzy to wash her face and hands, then went out to the American diner Izzy liked.

'They have a special ice-cream machine here where you make your own sundae,' Izzy told him, and pointed out the line of people queuing up to make their own sundaes. 'Can we?'

Marc looked to Laurie for guidance; at her nod, he said, 'Sure, if you have room after your dinner.'

When they'd finished their main course, Izzy looked expectantly at them both.

'Sorry, I don't have room for a pudding,' Laurie said, patting her stomach.

Izzy's face fell. 'Oh.'

'I do.' Marc smiled at the little girl. 'How about you and I make a sundae together and share it?'

She beamed at him in reply.

Five minutes later they'd reached the head of the queue for the ice-cream machine. Marc turned out to be very adept at swirling the ice cream round so it made a huge mountain. Izzy added plenty of rainbow-coloured sprinkles and mini chocolate flakes, and together they went back to join Laurie with their creation.

Marc nearly teased Laurie for being predictable when she took a photograph of him and Izzy with their spoons poised just above their dessert, grinning conspiratorially.

When they'd finished, Izzy gave him a spontaneous hug and said, 'I'm glad you're my friend. You make the most brilliant ice-cream sundaes, and this is one of the *best* times I've ever been here.'

'Me, too,' he said easily.

'It's the *only* time you've ever been here,' Izzy pointed out.

'It's still the best,' Marc told her with a grin.

Though he didn't quite dare meet Laurie's eyes, not sure what he'd see there. And not wanting to think about what he'd like to see there. He really wasn't ready to take this another step forward, and he was pretty sure she wasn't either

To avoid the awkwardness, he turned the conversation back to ice cream and favourite flavours. And only then he did look at Laurie, relieved to see that she was laughing and her expression was light rather than intense.

Late on Monday afternoon, Laurie's phone beeped, signalling a text message.

Am home now. Come round any time you like.

A thrill ran through her. It was crazy, but Marc made her feel as if she was eighteen years old again. And she'd even dressed up a little, the way she would've done for a date in her teens.

Because this counted as a date.

And Marc obviously noticed, because he kissed her lingeringly when he closed the front door behind her. 'You look gorgeous—not that you don't usually, but…well, I'm not used to seeing you in a skirt.' He kissed her again. 'And you have very nice legs, Dr Grant.'

Pleased, she smiled at him and kissed him back. 'Thank you.'

'Would you like some coffee? Or something cold?' he asked.

'It's baking out there. Something cold would be lovely, please.'

He fetched them both a glass of chilled sparkling water with ice and slice of lime.

'Perfect.' She took a grateful sip.

'Come and sit down.' He ushered her into his living room.

She looked around, frowning slightly. 'Something's different about your house, though I can't put my finger on it. Hang on, do I spy things on your shelves? Clutter? Tut, tut, what happened to Dr Neat Freak?' she teased.

'I just unpacked a few things.'

She raised an eyebrow. 'Indeed. You have books, you have films, you have music…' She browsed along his shelves. 'So you're a big sci fi fan.'

''Fraid so,' he teased.

'When did you do all this?'

'Last weekend.' He touched the backs of his fingers to her cheek. 'Spending the day with you and Izzy gave me a bit of backbone, and I finally felt brave enough to face it—all except one box,' he admitted.

'One box?'

He swallowed hard. 'Photographs.'

She took his hand. 'And would I be right in guessing that they've been packed away since well before you moved?'

He nodded. 'We used to have nearly as many photographs as you do around the house, but after Ginny died I felt bad every time I saw them. I packed them away to stop myself going crazy with guilt. I put them in a box quite a while before I decided to move away from London, and I haven't looked at them since. Which also makes me feel bad.' He sighed. 'I know I'm going to have to face them eventually.'

'How about now? When you've got someone to keep you company?'

'I can't ask you to do that.'

'Of course you can.' She reached up to kiss him. 'It's not just about the hot monkey sex, you know. We're friends, too. And you'd do the same for me.'

He thought about it. 'Yes.' And, because it put the moment of reckoning off for just a little longer, he asked, 'Do you have pictures of Izzy's father around the house?'

'That's a bit of a tricky one.' She sighed. 'If Dean had wanted to be part of Izzy's life—well, I guess we wouldn't have split up in the first place, because he wouldn't have run away from his fear of being a father by having an affair and then leaving it to me to make the decision to end our relationship. But if he'd simply fallen out of love with me and in love with someone else, and had still wanted to be part of Izzy's life, then obviously for her sake I'd still have pictures of him around the house.' She shrugged. 'But he doesn't want to be part of her life. So, no, I don't have pictures of him around.'

'Does Izzy ever ask about him?'

'Thankfully, no. I guess I'm a bit of a coward,

because I still haven't worked out how to tell her that he doesn't want to know her. I don't want her to feel rejected or abandoned. I want her to know that she's loved very, very much—but it's a hard thing to do, to tell a child that one of her parents just doesn't want to know. I did think about telling her that he died when she was a baby—but that wouldn't be fair, because then I'd have to tell her the truth when she's older, and a lie that big would do an awful lot of damage to her.' She bit her lip. 'Right now, she's too young to understand just how complicated people are, so I fudge the issue, and luckily I'm not the only single parent in the school so she doesn't feel that she's different.'

'From what I can see, you're doing a great job,' Marc said, meaning it. 'And I'm in the camp that thinks Dean needed his head examined. A talented, caring, lovely woman like you and a beautiful child—he was a fool to let you both go.'

And, although Marc still hadn't worked out how to tell her the whole truth about the accident, he was talking from experience. As a man who'd been every bit as much of a fool and had let everything good in his life go.

Maybe working through the photographs with her would help him find the right words to tell her the rest of his past.

'Are you sure you don't mind helping me?' he asked again.

'Of course I'm sure.'

He fetched the last box from the dining room, and carried it into the kitchen. Once he'd set it on the table and sliced open the tape, he stopped. Unpacking his life. His memories. All the things he'd lost.

He felt slightly sick.

'Marc, remember the story about Pandora?' she said softly.

'No.' Well, he sort of did. Half-remembered. But at that precise moment his head felt as if it had frozen and he couldn't think of anything.

'She opened a box. It was full of scary stuff. But, right at the bottom, there was hope.'

Hope.

That was what Laurie was offering him. A future even.

He undid the flaps of the box.

Right at the top was a photograph from his wedding day; the silver frame was slightly tarnished and needed polishing. The sight of it sent a throb of guilt through him.

As if she guessed what was wrong, she said softly, 'A silver polishing cloth will sort that out in a couple of minutes. Don't beat yourself up about this.' She smiled at him. 'Ginny was a gorgeous bride.'

His voice sounded rusty as he replied, 'Yes.' Ginny was classically pretty, with blonde hair she'd worn in an elegant chignon and clear grey eyes. There was a huge lump in his throat as he stared at the photograph. 'We'd only known each other for six months when we got married.'

'A whirlwind romance,' she said lightly.

'Something like that. We met at a party, a friend of a friend, and we just hit it off.'

He took the next photo out of the box: one of Ginny sitting reading in their garden when he'd called her name and she'd looked up at him over the edge of her book. It was one of his favourites, the one he'd kept on his desk at work in his old practice.

'She looks nice as well as beautiful,' Laurie said.

'She was. Everyone who knew her liked her.

She was the sort who never had a bad word to say about anyone.' He smiled. 'I'm not going to say we never had a fight—that'd be totally unrealistic—but they were never bad fights. They were always over something little and stupid, and we made up quickly.'

When he took the next photo frame out and set it on the table, Laurie said, 'They look so much like you, they have to be your parents.'

'Yes. This one was taken at the wedding. My dad's a chemistry teacher, a bit of a mad professor type. Getting him in an ordinary suit takes a lot, and to get him into morning dress...' He gave her a rueful smile. 'Well, Ginny talked him into it.'

Next was a woman in a graduation photo. 'Your little sister?' Laurie guessed.

'Yvonne. Vonnie. Yes. She's up in Glasgow.' She swallowed. 'She's a primary school teacher. I haven't seen her for months.' He sighed. 'I really ought to make the effort and go up to see her.'

'But it was easier to keep your distance from people who'd known Ginny and would bring back all the memories?' Laurie asked softly.

How could she understand that so easily? 'Yes.'

He took a photo album out of the box, but he couldn't quite face opening it and seeing all the memories on the pages.

And then a loose folder slipped out of the album onto the table.

It was small, square, glossy and white, and Marc knew that Laurie would realise exactly what it was. He sucked in a breath. He was going to have to tell her now, even though he wasn't ready and didn't have the right words.

And it felt as if someone had just opened his chest, reached in and was squeezing his heart.

CHAPTER TEN

LAURIE recognised the type of folder instantly. She had one of those herself, tucked into Izzy's baby book.

Marc hadn't said anything about having children.

But now she had a horrible, horrible feeling that she knew why. And why he'd been so antsy around Izzy at first.

Because he must have lost a child.

And, difficult as it was to face, she knew they both had to face it. Pussyfooting around the truth would be the quickest way to let misunderstandings happen. 'That's a scan picture,' she said softly.

'Yes.' Marc closed his eyes. 'I should have told you before now. I just didn't have the right words to tell you the worst bit.' He blew out a breath. 'So I guess I owe you the whole truth this time. I'm sorry I didn't prepare you better. And I'll understand if...' His voice tailed off as if he couldn't bear to say any more.

But she knew him well enough now to be able to guess what he meant. He'd understand if she didn't want to see him any more.

'Don't build a bridge to trouble,' she said.

He opened his eyes again, looking tortured. 'Ginny was...' He stopped, as if the words were choking him, and his voice was hoarse when he resumed. 'She was pregnant when she was killed. We'd only had the dating scan three days before.'

So he hadn't just lost his wife, he'd lost his unborn child as well, Laurie thought. She remembered her own scan with Izzy; she'd been alone because Dean hadn't wanted to be there. Part of her had been thrilled to see the new life growing inside her, and part of her had worried that Dean would never come to terms with it. And he hadn't; he'd missed out on everything because he wasn't interested. Whereas Marc had been there at the scan for his baby; he'd missed out everything because it had been taken from him. Her heart ached for him.

'We hadn't told anyone about the baby. We

wanted to wait until Ginny was at least twelve weeks and we'd had the scan. It felt like tempting fate to say anything before then,' Marc said. 'We'd planned to have both families over to our place the following weekend. We told them it was just because it was summer and we thought it'd be nice to get together. And we were so looking forward to telling our parents that they were going to be grandparents.' He dragged in a breath. 'But Ginny never got to do that. She never got the fuss she deserved from her mum and dad. I took that from her.'

Marc looked as if he was drowning in misery, and Laurie felt guilty for pushing him. He hadn't wanted to face the photographs, and now she could see why. It had clearly ripped the top off all his scars, and he was hurting again as if it had only just happened.

She wrapped her arms round him and held him close. 'It wasn't you that took it from her, it was the accident. Nothing about this was deliberate. And the accident took the baby from you, too. As well as the woman you loved. You're just as much a victim of this as she was.'

'I just wish I'd taken better care of her.'

'Nobody can change the past,' she said softly. 'You've been holding onto this for two years, Marc. Don't you think it's time you let go of the bad feelings and forgave yourself?'

He said nothing.

'Ginny loved you as much as you loved her, right?'

He nodded.

'So would she want to see you ripping your heart out like this?' Laurie asked. 'Would she want to see you drowning in misery and guilt?'

'I suppose not.'

'Exactly.' She paused. 'And you could always try looking at it the other way round. Supposing you'd been the one behind the steering-wheel when that other driver was on the wrong side of the road? Supposing you'd been killed and she'd walked away without a scratch? She would've been left to bring up the baby on her own. A single parent. Don't get me wrong—I don't regret having Izzy for a minute, not a single second, and she brings such joy to my life. But being a single parent isn't easy. Even if you have close family who'll support you and help out with babysitting, at the end of the day all the responsibilities are yours, and yours alone. You don't have someone to share the worries with, someone to talk over decisions with. You just have to hope that you're doing the right thing and then try not to beat yourself up about it if it turns out that you did the wrong thing. You have to recognise that you did your best at the time, and that expecting more of yourself in hindsight just isn't fair to anyone.'

He swallowed hard. 'I guess so.'

'On top of all that, would you have wanted Ginny to grieve for you for the rest of her life, forgetting all the good times you had together and only focusing on the stuff you didn't have time to do together?'

He was silent for a long, long time. 'No, of course not. I'd want her to be happy. To find someone else who'd love her as much as I did.'

'I didn't know her, but I'd guess that you married someone with as generous a spirit as you have. You need to forgive yourself, Marc, for her sake. Let yourself remember the good times without torturing yourself with might-have-beens.'

'I don't even know if we were going to have a

boy or a girl—it was too early to tell—and…'
He blew out a breath. 'He or she would've been
a toddler now. Twenty months. Walking, just
starting to chatter.'

'That's why you find it hard to be around children, outside work?'

He nodded. 'But your Izzy…she's so like you.
Warm and sweet and accepting. And what she
said on Saturday night…'

Laurie held him close. 'She meant it. She
really likes you.'

'That's why I didn't want to get close to anyone. Because I'm terrified of making another
mistake like that, letting someone else down.'
He looked her straight in the eye. 'I'm scared of
letting *you* down.'

'I've already been there,' she said, 'and I can
tell you now that you're nothing like Dean. If
anything, you're too far the other way and you're
holding yourself responsible for things that nobody else would hold you responsible for.'

'Ginny's parents do,' he said. 'They blame me.
They said I should've been driving—I knew she
was pregnant, and I should've looked after her
better.'

'That's grief talking. Pain. And you were there with her at the end, so that makes you the one it's easiest for them to lash out at,' she said.

'I took their only child away from them. Their grandchild. Their future.'

'Not you. The accident,' she said again. 'There's a difference. And I only wish I could make you see it.'

She stared at him, feeling frustrated and helpless. He was so unhappy, blaming himself and not letting himself see what he still had left in his life. Not letting himself see the hope. How could she reach him, make him realise that it wasn't his fault?

She reached up to kiss him, and the kiss turned heated as Marc responded, clearly needing the warmth that she could give him.

Laurie wasn't quite sure how they'd got there—whether he'd carried her or they'd stumbled together, still kissing and wrapped in each other—but the next thing she knew they were in his bed, skin to skin, and her arms were tightly round him as he entered her.

Afterwards, he held her close. 'I'm sorry, that wasn't fair of me.'

'Don't feel guilty. I was with you all the way.' She pressed a kiss against his bare shoulder.

'What's that noise?' he asked, frowning.

She listened, and recognised the tone instantly. 'The alarm on my phone. Which means I need to go and collect Izzy from Molly's mum.'

'Oh, help, and I didn't cook dinner for you as I promised. I'm sorry. I've been really selfish.'

'No, you haven't. It's OK. I'm not desperately hungry, and I can make myself an omelette or something later.' She touched his face and smiled. 'I think there was something else we both needed a little more than food.'

'Thank you. For understanding. For not judging.'

'Of course I'm not going to judge you. I'm not perfect. Nobody is.' She kissed him lightly and scrambled out of bed. 'I'd better get dressed. I'll see you tomorrow. But you can't change the past, Marc. You can only learn from it and make the future better. And remember what I said about Pandora. There was hope left in the box. You still have that. You just need to let yourself see it.'

* * *

On Wednesday evening, Laurie came home after seeing Marc.

'Did you have a good evening, Laurie?' Diane asked.

'Yes. Tonight was badminton.' She laughed. 'There are people who can do racquet sports, and then there's me, so although I joined in I was pretty rubbish. But some of the patients seemed to enjoy it, so I'm crossing my fingers that the badminton club might set up a beginners' league for them.'

'That's good.' Diane paused. 'How was Dr Bailey?'

'Fine.'

'So it was a good debriefing meeting, then?'

Laurie felt her eyes narrow. 'Is something wrong, Mum?'

'No. But your eyes are very sparkly tonight, love.'

Laurie frowned. 'No, they're not.'

'And you've been smiling an awful lot more lately,' Diane mused.

'I have no idea what you mean.'

Diane looked thoughtful. 'In fact, anyone looking at you right now might think that you've recently been very thoroughly kissed.'

Laurie's hands flew to her face. She could feel her cheeks heating and knew that her face was bright red—and not from the badminton session either. 'I don't know what to say.'

'You're entitled to have some fun in your life, love. And Izzy likes him.'

Laurie gave up trying to pretend that she didn't know who her mother was talking about. 'How do you know?'

'She was telling me about him today—how he's your friend from work and he's new, like Molly in her class, so you're being kind and letting him go out with the two of you and Cocoa. Apparently, Cocoa likes him, too.'

The dog wagged his tail, as if to confirm it.

Laurie squirmed. 'Mum, I don't date loads of men and introduce Iz to a new "uncle" every week.'

'I know you don't, love.'

'And Marc's a nice guy.' Laurie took a deep breath. 'As far as she's concerned, we're just friends. Like her and Molly.'

'He lost his wife, didn't he? That's so sad, to lose someone so young.'

'Mmm,' Laurie said noncommittally. She wasn't going to betray any of Marc's confidences.

'So are your father and I going to meet him?'

Laurie blew out a breath. 'Mum, we're not dating officially.'

'Just unofficially.'

'We're taking it slowly,' Laurie said.

'All right. This Sunday. Lunch at one.'

'He might not be free.'

Diane smiled. 'I think he will be. Talk him into it. And if that doesn't work, kiss him into it. It's what I do with your father.'

Laurie groaned. 'Mum, that's way too much information!'

Diane just laughed and hugged her. 'It's time you met someone nice. Someone who'll treat you a lot better than Dean did. And children and dogs tend to be good judges of character. If Izzy and Cocoa like him, that's a good thing.'

'And that's not enough for you?' Laurie asked helplessly.

'No. I want to meet him properly.'

* * *

The following morning, Laurie sent Marc a text: *Houston, we have a problem. Need to talk.*

His reply came straight back: *Duck pond at lunch?*

Perfect.

Tina raised her eyebrows at them in the patisserie. 'Lunching together again, Dr Grant and Dr Bailey? People will start to talk, you know.'

'We're discussing the project,' Laurie said loftily. 'Talking of which, did you give your mum the schedule?'

'Yes. And thanks for that; she's cheered up a bit. I think she's going to come on Wednesday night, though she's—well, she's being totally daft. She's worried about being the new girl.'

Laurie smiled. 'She'll know absolutely everyone there, so she won't count as new. Trust me, she'll enjoy it.'

They paid for their sandwiches, then headed for the duck pond.

'So what's the problem?' Marc asked.

'We've been rumbled,' she said.

He frowned. 'How do you mean?'

'Mum guessed. Last night. She, um, said that I looked as if I'd been kissed. Very thoroughly.'

'Ah. So we need to cool it?'

'Not exactly. But she's expecting you to arrive for Sunday lunch at one o'clock.'

For a moment, she thought he was going to make an excuse.

Then he nodded. 'OK. I'm driving. I'll pick you up at…how far away do your parents live?'

'Ten minutes from me. Your side of the village.'

'Twenty to one, then. To give us some wriggle room.'

'OK.' She could guess exactly why he wanted to drive; it would give him an excuse not to drink, without having to explain why.

Laurie felt incredibly nervous on the Sunday— more so even than the first time she'd taken Dean to meet her parents. This was going to be an important milestone. What if they didn't like Marc? She was pretty sure that wouldn't be the case—Marc had nice manners, plus he was genuinely one of the good guys—but, even so, the worry was there.

He arrived at twenty-five to one, and she put Izzy's seat in the back of his car.

'No, Cocoa, you can't come with us because you know Smudge won't like it,' Izzy told the dog solemnly.

'Who's Smudge?' Marc asked.

'Nanna and Granddad's cat. She's called Smudge because she's white and she has a big grey smudge across her nose.'

'Ah, right.' Marc handed Laurie a gorgeous bouquet of flowers.

'How lovely,' she said.

He smiled. 'Sorry, Dr Grant, they're not actually for you—but I was hoping perhaps you could look after them while I'm driving.'

He'd thought to buy her mother flowers. Laurie's heart swelled. Yes, this was going to work out. Even though right at this moment he looked even more nervous than she did. 'She'll love them,' she said softly. 'And she'll like you.'

Marc didn't look convinced, and climbed into the driving seat.

Laurie directed him to her parents' house. As Izzy ran down the garden path to knock on the front door, she said softly, 'I'm sorry about this.

I don't want it to be an ordeal for you—and we can leave any time you like. Give me the nod, and I'll do a fake call on my phone and say it's a patient.'

'Thank you.' He gave her a wry smile. 'Ginny's parents loathe me, but I guess they have a reason—yours don't.'

'Yet' was written all over his face.

She squeezed his hand briefly. 'It's going to be fine.'

Her parents were already at the door, waiting for them.

Laurie introduced them swiftly. 'Mum, Dad, this is Marc, my new colleague at the practice and brilliant co-coordinator of my pet project. Marc, these are my parents, Diane and Roderick Grant.'

Marc handed the flowers to Diane and a bottle of wine to Roderick.

'How lovely—thank you, Marc. Come and sit down,' Diane said, 'while I put these in water.'

'I'll come with you, Mum—Izzy and I made some cakes,' Laurie said.

'Can I get you a glass of wine, Marc?' Roderick asked.

'No, thanks—I'm driving,' Marc explained. 'But coffee or a soft drink would be lovely— whatever's easiest.'

'Fair enough.' Roderick looked approving, clearly relieved that Marc wasn't going to put his daughter and granddaughter at risk.

When they sat down in the living room, the cat came over and sniffed at him, then curled on his lap.

Diane stared at him in surprise. 'Smudge doesn't usually go anywhere near men except Roderick. She was badly treated as a kitten. But she obviously likes you.'

'So does Cocoa—so do I,' Izzy piped up.

'And I like you and Cocoa too, Iz.' Marc made a fuss of the cat and smiled. 'So Smudge is a rescue cat? Now I know where Laurie gets her rescuing tendencies from.'

The conversation was easy over lunch, and Diane allowed Marc to help clear the table, though she shooed him out of the kitchen. 'You don't have to wash up. That's what dishwashers are for.'

They sat in the garden after lunch. Marc wasn't that surprised when Laurie's brother Joe, sister-in-law Rose and their children dropped in during the middle of the afternoon, saying that they were 'just passing'. He'd expected to be under scrutiny by the whole family—and he could understand why. Laurie had been hurt in the past and they'd want to be sure that whoever she was seeing would treat her properly.

But the atmosphere stayed relaxed and easy, and Izzy had a whale of a time running around the garden with her cousins. Marc was surprised to discover that he was enjoying himself, too. But at the same time it scared him. This was almost too perfect, too good to be true. Laurie's family were accepting him as easily as Ginny's family had. And yet it had gone so badly wrong with Ginny. What was to say that this wasn't going to go wrong, too? Part of him wanted to back away before that could happen.

And yet Laurie had already been badly let down. He didn't want to hurt her. He was going to have to be very, very careful.

When Marc drove Laurie and Izzy home later that evening, her phone beeped several times. He didn't ask, and she didn't look at the texts;

but he could make an educated guess who they were from and what the subject was.

'Marc, will you read me my bedtime story tonight, please?' Izzy asked.

He knew he ought to make an excuse. Back off. Yet how could he resist those big brown eyes and that hopeful smile?

She persuaded him into reading her three stories, and then Laurie came up to kiss her goodnight.

'One more story? Please?' the little girl asked hopefully.

'No. You've had lots of stories from Marc already tonight. It's time to go to sleep now, or you'll be too tired at school tomorrow to play with Georgia and Molly,' Laurie said.

Izzy thought about it, then nodded and wriggled back under her covers. Though not until she'd had a kiss goodnight from both Laurie and Marc.

'I hope today wasn't too much of a trial,' Laurie said quietly when they went downstairs.

'No. Your family's lovely. They're very like you,' Marc said.

'They liked you, too. That's what the phone barrage was about.'

'I thought my ears were burning,' he said drily.

She laughed and kissed him. 'Mum says you're a sweetie, Rose says you're a keeper, and my brother wants to know your secret because the cat will never let Joe pick him up but was all over you.'

'So does that mean we're going public now?'

'Not quite—I've asked them to keep it to themselves for the time being. Though Mum will no doubt be talking to Fiona.' She rolled her eyes. 'Actually, I'm a bit surprised that she and Jay didn't "accidentally" call in as well as Joe and Rose this afternoon. Mum and Fiona have been having this campaign for months to make me date someone.' She laughed. 'They were even going to sign me up on a dating site until I had a hissy fit on them.'

'Hmm.' Marc paused. 'I guess you could meet my family. If you liked.'

She nodded. 'I'd like that.'

'It's time I invited them down. Maybe you could come for Sunday lunch?'

'That'd be great.' She kissed him. 'I just

hope—well, that they won't mind me being a single parent. And that they won't think I'm using you.'

'They won't. And once they've met you and Izzy… Well, I think you'll bring as much of a sparkle to their lives as you do to mine.'

She held her breath. Was Marc about to declare himself?

She knew how she was beginning to feel about him, and she hoped that he felt the same way. That the fears about it all going wrong were starting to fade and he could see a potential future with her.

But when he moved the conversation onto a different topic, Laurie knew that she'd just have to stay patient for a little longer. Until he was ready.

CHAPTER ELEVEN

'THE project,' Marc said when he and Laurie were eating their sandwiches by the duck pond on Monday lunchtime, 'might just have notched up its first success.'

'Who?'

'Mrs Reynolds. I saw her about her results today, and she's going to try exercise and life-style changes and review it again in a month. Obviously she gave me permission to tell you this.' He smiled. 'She's signed up to join the gym.'

'Neil's?'

He nodded. 'She, um, has similar views about him to yours. But apparently they offer one-to-one personal training sessions and some of the trainers are female. She's booking in appoint-ments on the way home from work so it makes her turn up for it, and she had her induction ses-sion last week.'

'That's brilliant news.'

'And she says she would never have done it if you hadn't asked her to go along to the Wednesday sessions.'

'I'm so pleased. This is the sort of thing that really makes our job worthwhile, knowing we've actually made a difference,' Laurie said, beaming at him.

'That's what I told her, Dr Fixit,' Marc said with a smile. 'And I said you'd be as pleased as I was.'

'I'm so going to give her a hug on Wednesday,' Laurie said. 'That's made my day.'

'It's a lovely house. Ginny—' Peggy Bailey stopped short and looked nervously at her son.

'Ginny would've loved it,' Marc finished. 'The garden, the fact it's old and full of character, the view.'

She looked at him in wonder. 'You actually said her name.'

'I can do that now.' It still made him ache inside, and he knew that he'd never quite stop missing her, but he was ready to move on.

'So you're really happy here?' Peggy asked.

'Your mother's worried about you,' Donald said. 'Because you moved a hundred miles away, among strangers. At least in London you knew people.'

'And I had too many memories,' Marc said gently. 'Here, it's a new start for me. I like the people I work with, I like the people around here, and I'm really enjoying my job.'

'That's good. All you need is—' Peggy bit back the words. 'Sorry. I won't say it.'

Marc smiled. 'It's OK, Mum. I know what you're going to say. All I need is to meet someone. Not to forget Ginny, but someone who'll help me move on.'

'Well, yes.' She gave him a hug. 'I'm sorry. I know you're thirty-five, not five, and you're very clever and you're capable of doing anything you choose—but I'm your mother. I can't help worrying about you.'

Just as Laurie worried about Izzy. 'I'm not going to give you a hard time about it, Mum.'

'I notice you've got your photographs up. You haven't had them out since—well…' she finished awkwardly.

'Since Ginny's funeral, when I took them

down because I couldn't face them. I know. And I shut you, Dad and Vonnie out afterwards. I'm sorry.' He blew out a breath. 'It was the only way I could cope and keep myself going.'

'You do look happier here,' Donald said.

'I am,' Marc said. And they'd meet the reasons why, very shortly.

He finished showing them round the house.

'The table's set for five,' Peggy noted as they reached the dining room.

'I was coming to that. I've invited a couple of people round—people I'd like you to meet.'

Peggy's eyes widened. 'Marc, are you seeing someone?'

'Yes, but it's complicated. Laurie and I are keeping it quiet at the moment. Not because we're ashamed of what we're doing, but because we're taking things gently and because she has her little girl to think of.'

'A little girl.' There was a film of tears in Peggy's eyes.

'Mum.' Marc hugged her. 'I know. But Izzy's older than…' He couldn't quite bring himself to say the words. 'She's five. And she's a sweetie. I'm pretty sure you'll both like them.'

'Do you love her?'

'I'm not ready to answer that one yet, Mum,' he said gently. 'But we'll see how it goes.'

A quarter of an hour before lunch, the doorbell rang. Marc ushered Laurie and Izzy inside and introduced them swiftly to his parents. 'Laurie, Izzy—these are my parents, Peggy and Donald Bailey. Mum, Dad, this is my friend and colleague Laurie Grant and her daughter Isobel—though everyone calls her Izzy.'

'We made you some special cakes for tea,' Izzy said.

'With lots of sprinkles, I hope,' Marc said.

She nodded. 'Lots and lots and lots. I did one with an M on it, 'specially for you.

He ruffled her hair. 'Thank you, sweetheart.'

Laurie had some idea of how nervous Marc had been about meeting her family, because she felt the same about meeting his. Although she'd always got on well with Dean's family, this was different, and she really hoped that Marc's parents wouldn't compare her to Ginny.

But Peggy and Donald turned out to be really easy to talk to. And they were naturals with children, she thought; Peggy asked Izzy about school, and taught her how to draw cats—a skill that Laurie knew Izzy was going to love sharing with Georgia and Molly.

'So you work together?' Peggy asked over lunch.

'Yes, and Marc's helping me out with my pet project—preventative medicine. It's aimed at people who are at risk of developing diabetes and heart conditions. We've been setting up taster exercise sessions and talks from experts, and so far the project's going really well. Even though the summer holidays are coming up, everyone's making an effort to be there on Wednesday nights.' She smiled at Peggy. 'That cat you drew for Izzy was amazing. Obviously I had to draw some diagrams, to get through med school, but it's not my strongest suit.'

'I was an art teacher, before I retired,' Peggy said.

'I like art,' Izzy chipped in. 'We made pottery hedgehogs at school. They're being cooked in a special oven at middle school next week, and then we're going to paint them. We all had to think of names starting with H. Mine's called Horatio.'

At teatime, Peggy and Donald were impressed with Izzy's sparkly cupcakes, and Laurie had to promise to email Peggy the recipe for her lemon cake.

Laurie was surprised at how quickly the time went. 'We have to go, young lady,' she said to Izzy.

'Already?'

'Yes, because I need to wash your hair tonight, and you know it takes ages to dry. Plus you've got school tomorrow.'

Izzy nodded. 'I've had a lovely time. Thank you for having us, Marc,' she said politely.

'My pleasure, Iz. And thank you for the cakes. Especially for my one.'

'My pleasure,' she echoed. 'It's the holidays soon, and Mummy says we can go to the beach and go swimming lots and lots.' She hugged him. 'Will you come crabbing with us again?'

'Sure I will. Come on, I'll give you a piggyback to the car.' He bent down so she could climb onto his back. 'Ready—one, two, three!'

* * *

When Laurie and Izzy had gone, Peggy said, 'They're lovely, both of them. And they both clearly think a lot of you.' She paused. 'Can I tell Vonnie?'

'I'd rather do that myself,' Marc said. 'I was thinking about inviting her here in the school holidays.'

'She'd love that,' Donald said.

'And I'm so glad to see you with a smile in your eyes again,' Peggy said. 'I missed that. And anyone who can put the smile back in your eyes is more than OK with me.'

Marc called Laurie later, after his parents had left. 'You made a hit with my parents.' He paused. 'I was thinking about asking my sister to stay in the school holidays. Would you be OK about meeting her?'

'Of course, and you're being nice and letting me meet everyone gradually. I'm afraid you got the whole lot of my family at once.'

'Well, they live nearby. Mine live a long way away.'

'I liked your mum and dad. So did Izzy; she says your mum has nice hair.'

He laughed. 'I'll tell her; she'll be pleased. I'll see you at work tomorrow.'

The middle of the month saw the twelve-week point of the project.

'Today's not so much an exercise session as a time to review how things are going and sort out another week of measuring your exercise levels and how they've changed,' Laurie said with a smile. 'Marc and I will be checking your weight, your blood pressure and taking a blood sample so the lab can tell us your cholesterol levels. Next week we'll be able to give you the overall group results, as well as giving you a private letter with your personal results.'

'And then it's the last week of the project,' Marc said. 'Which I guess might make it easier for some of you, as it's almost the end of term.'

There were general groans. 'Can we extend the project?' Frank Riley asked. 'Because I'm really enjoying this and I don't want to stop.'

'Me neither,' Judy Reynolds agreed. 'I'm feeling much better than I was three months ago. And I'm definitely doing more exercise.'

'I'm walking my neighbour's dog for her,' Peter Jackson chipped in.

'And I'm eating better. I did a food diary, and I couldn't believe how much I was eating between meals. I don't now,' Carrie Baker said. 'And I eat a lot more fish. I didn't think I liked fish, but once you've used a few herbs and spices...well, it's not so bad.'

'Carrie, I've got a really good recipe for sweet chili salmon,' Judy Reynolds said. 'I'll write it down for you and bring it next week.'

'They've really gelled as a group,' Laurie said when she and Marc were packing everything away at the end of a session. 'I love the way they're swapping recipes and encouraging each other.'

'And they want to continue,' Marc said.

'There was some research I read, a couple of years back, that it takes just over two months on average to form a habit—obviously it depends on what the habit is, because some things in the study took longer and some took a lot less. I guess we've got them into the exercise habit. But it'd be a shame to pull the support away now,' Laurie said. 'Would you mind keeping it going for a bit longer—say, until the end of the school holidays?'

He stole a kiss. 'That's fine with me, Dr Fixit.'

'Great. I'll sort out the hall booking tomorrow.'

'And then maybe next week we can find out which of the activities they liked best and see if we can get those people back for more sessions,' Marc suggested.

'Good idea.' She smiled at him. 'I've really loved doing this. It's made a difference.'

'And we work well as a team.' Marc held her gaze. 'We're good together, Laurie.'

And she had the distinct feeling that he didn't just mean professionally. Which was good, because that was how she was beginning to feel about him, too. It was scary, thinking about trusting someone—but she knew he wasn't Dean. He wouldn't let her down. Wouldn't abandon her.

But she wouldn't push just yet. Taking it slowly was working just fine for both of them.

The following week, they collected in the monitors.

'I've got your individual results here,' Laurie said, 'but I'd like to tell you how you've done as a group. On average, you've lost more than ten pounds each, your blood pressure has improved by ten points, your resting pulse is down by five beats a minute and your cholesterol levels are down one and a half points. Obviously, that's an average, but I don't want any of you to feel disappointed with how you've done, because *all* of you are showing an improvement in your health.'

'And we're happy to keep the sessions going until the end of the summer holidays, if you are,' Marc said.

'Absolutely!' Judy Reynolds said with a grin. 'And we really appreciate it, Dr Bailey.'

'Good, because now we want to know which activities you enjoyed most, so we can get people back again,' Marc said. 'And, if enough of you are interested, we might be able to get some beginners' classes sorted out for the start of the new term.'

The summer, Laurie thought, was one of the best she could ever remember. The sun seemed to shine every day; being school holidays, she was able to spend more time with Izzy, and sneak in more time with Marc as well.

Yvonne, Marc's sister, came to stay with Marc for a week; Laurie liked her instantly, and Izzy adored her to the point where she asked if Yvonne could come to be the new teacher at school, because Mrs Richards was leaving to have a baby.

It was the happiest Laurie had ever been. Now Marc had opened up to her, she was falling in love with him. She loved his dry sense of humour, his willingness to spend time with Izzy, the way he was good with her dog and her parents' rescue cat.

Marc Bailey was the kind of man she'd always dreamed of being with. Patient, kind and loving. Her family liked him, and his family liked her.

Perhaps it was time to talk to Izzy, to see how she'd feel about Marc taking a bigger role in their lives. Time that she stopped being a coward and worrying that it was all going to go wrong.

Because what could go wrong?

The following week, when term had started again, Laurie felt a bit queasy. She knew there weren't any sicky bugs doing the rounds; Izzy seemed fine, so it probably wasn't anything she'd eaten or Izzy would've been complaining of feeling sick, too. And there was a metallic taste in her mouth.

Or maybe it was the pine nuts she'd had in the pesto the other night. She'd had a couple of patients coming in saying that everything tasted awful, and one of them had brought in an article about 'pine mouth'. It seemed that the taste disturbance occurred a couple of days after you'd eaten pine nuts and lasted for a couple of weeks, but other than that there was no lasting harm. Well, she'd just avoid pine nuts for a while and put up with it.

But the day after that her bra felt uncomfortable and her breasts were sore.

If it wasn't for the fact that Laurie had had her period as normal last month, she'd think she was pregnant.

Which was totally ridiculous. She and Marc had used condoms. Of course she couldn't be pregnant.

Or could she? Now she thought about it, her last period had been a bit on the light side. And there had been one time where a condom had broken; she'd meant to do something about the morning-after pill, but had forgotten.

Oh, help.

Izzy hadn't been a planned baby either.

Just supposing…?

She couldn't get the idea out of her head all day. No way could she get a test from the pharmacy attached to the surgery; she didn't want anyone to know about this. In the end, she drove five miles away to the supermarket; and, just to make sure she didn't see anyone she knew who might glance into her basket and see what she was buying, she covered the test with a newspaper until she reached the self-service tills, and ran the test over the bar code reader as quickly as possible.

Luckily Tina had invited Izzy and Molly to tea with Georgia, so Laurie didn't have to wait until Izzy was asleep before doing the test. She drove home, went to the bathroom, did the test, and waited.

One blue line appeared in the test window, to tell her it had worked.

She kept looking at the window, with one eye on the second hand of her watch to check the time. After two minutes there was no second line. She breathed a sigh of relief. Of course she wasn't pregnant. This was obviously some weird kind of bug.

She turned away to wash her hands, then took some toilet paper to wrap round the test, intending to bury it at the bottom of the bin.

She stopped dead.

Somehow, when she'd looked away, another blue line had appeared on the test.

How? How could it just have appeared out of nowhere?

Especially as it wasn't even a faint line—it was a wide, strong line.

The test was positive. Very, very positive.

She was pregnant.

CHAPTER TWELVE

LAURIE went cold.

Pregnant.

She closed the lid on the toilet seat and sat down, wrapping her arms around herself, but the cold feeling wouldn't go away.

Pregnant.

And this wasn't a planned baby.

This was where her life had all gone wrong last time. When she'd found out that she was accidentally pregnant, it had signalled the end of her relationship with Dean.

OK, so Marc was nothing like Dean; but she knew he had issues about children. He'd looked broken inside when he'd told her about the un-born baby he'd lost in the accident. Would the news of her pregnancy bring everything back to him and make him crumble? Was she put-ting her trust in someone who wouldn't be able to cope with a baby—the same mistake she'd made before?

Marc seemed to have grown close to Izzy, but that was different. This was a pregnancy. It would bring back difficult memories for him—memories of the scan he'd gone to with Ginny, the accident, and everything he'd lost. Laurie couldn't help panicking that everything was going to go wrong when he found out.

She had to find a way to tell him. But right at that moment she had absolutely no idea how to break the news. How to soften it. How he'd react.

She made excuses to avoid him at work; and on the Wednesday night she claimed she had a headache, saying that she needed an early night and maybe they could catch up on the project later.

And please, please, let her find the right way of telling him that she was pregnant with his baby.

Something was wrong with Laurie, Marc was sure. He wasn't the paranoid sort, but she was definitely avoiding him, both at work and outside.

He didn't have a clue what was wrong, and his imagination was working overtime. Was she ill? Maybe she didn't want to worry him?

Or had she decided that she didn't want to take their relationship any further, and was slowly freezing him out? Though he didn't think that was her style; Laurie was direct about everything. She hated people pussyfooting about, and said that was the quickest way for misunderstandings to happen and cause problems.

When she'd made the excuse of yet another headache on the Friday night, Marc decided that enough was enough. He went to the supermarket and bought the nicest bouquet available: pink gerberas; purple sweet-scented stocks; white carnations; and white roses with the most delicate pink edging. Flowers he knew she'd adore. And hopefully they would persuade her to talk to him.

He knew Izzy would be in bed at this time of night. He didn't want Cocoa to bark madly and wake the little girl, so instead of knocking on the front door he rang Laurie's mobile.

She sounded wary. 'Marc?'

'We need to talk,' he said. 'I know Izzy's asleep, so rather than me ringing the bell and making the dog bark his head off, can you let me in?'

'Where are you?'

'Outside. In my car. And I'm not budging until you let me in and talk to me.'

He heard her sigh. 'OK.'

He'd locked his car door and was waiting outside by the time she undid the front door. He handed her the flowers.

'They're lovely, but you didn't need to buy me flowers.'

'Yes, I did,' he corrected. 'Something's wrong, Laurie. I don't know if it's something I've done or said, or something I've omitted to do or say— but something's wrong and I'm totally clueless about it. Talk to me. Tell me what's wrong, and we can fix it.'

She bit her lip. 'It's not exactly something you can fix.'

He felt his eyes widen. 'You're ill?'

'No.'

He blew out a breath. 'Thank God for that. I

was worried you were sick. Though, obviously, if you were, I'd support you and do whatever I could to help.'

She shook her head. 'It's not that.'

He had to face this head on. 'Or that you'd changed your mind about us and didn't want to see me any more, except as a colleague.'

She bit her lip. 'No-o.'

Her expression and the tone of her voice didn't bode well. He took a deep breath. 'OK. Hit me with it.'

'Come and sit down in the kitchen while I put these in water.'

He noticed that she hadn't offered him a drink, and that definitely wasn't usual behaviour for Laurie. She was clearly nerving herself to tell him something but what, he had absolutely no idea. She'd said that she hadn't changed her mind about them—or had she changed her mind and didn't know how to tell him?

He waited until she'd finished fiddling with the flowers.

And then, finally, she sat down opposite him. Not next to him or on his lap, he noticed, but opposite him.

This wasn't going to be good.

'There isn't an easy way to say this, Marc.'

Right. So she *was* breaking up with him.

He did his best to keep his voice neutral. 'So don't try to make it easy. Give it to me straight.'

She took a deep breath. 'I'm pregnant.'

Pregnant?

With his baby?

Marc felt as if someone had just punched him hard in the gut, and he couldn't breathe.

She was pregnant.

The last time he'd had news like this, he'd been thrilled to bits. He and Ginny had tried for a baby for six months, and Ginny had been worrying that maybe something was wrong because several of her friends had fallen pregnant the first month they'd tried. He'd been so pleased. So looking forward to having their baby, seeing the first smile and hearing the first giggle and the first word.

And then his life had gone into meltdown.

This wasn't the same. It wasn't remotely the same. He and Laurie weren't married—they weren't even a couple, as far as most of the outside world knew—and they hadn't been trying for a baby. There was no reason to think that his life would be hit by the same tragedy twice over.

But right now all he could see was the car coming towards them. Hear the crash. Glass splintering. The scrape of metal on metal. Ginny's head going forward. Everything echoey and muffled, as if he was under deep water. All in slow motion, as if he was living through it all again and this time he was even more powerless because he knew exactly what was going to happen and he couldn't do a thing to stop it.

Bile rose in his throat. He couldn't deal with this. Not here. Not now.

'I need some air,' he said, pushed his chair back, and left.

Laurie was too numb to move. But she heard the front door close quietly behind Marc.

He'd gone.

And she'd made the same mistake all over again. She'd fallen for a man who couldn't commit to her. She'd fallen for a man who didn't want a child. Who'd walked out on her.

True, Marc wasn't Dean. He hadn't been unfaithful to her or ignored Izzy.

But he'd still abandoned her as soon as she'd told him that she was pregnant. Just as Dean had when she'd told him the news. Yet again she'd put her trust in the wrong man.

'I'm such an idiot,' she said.

Cocoa put his paws on her knee and licked her face.

That was when the tears finally came. Laurie wrapped her arms round the dog, buried her face in his fur, and sobbed.

She'd known that Marc would find the news difficult to take. He'd lost his unborn child in the accident, along with Ginny, so of course the idea of a new baby would bring all that grief to the forefront.

Though she'd thought—*hoped*—that he'd be able to push it aside and focus on the fact that they were having a baby. That they could have a future together, as a family. Izzy had bonded with him, her family liked him, and his family liked her. They had a real chance of making this thing between them work.

But obviously Marc was never going to get over the past. Not that she would ever expect him to sweep his memories of Ginny into a mental box, never to be opened again—that would be wrong, because he'd loved his wife and she was part of his past, part of what had shaped him as a man. Laurie had really hoped that he could find it within himself to move on. That he felt enough for her to be able to leave his sadness behind and just remember the good bits about his past.

The night air wasn't cool. It was sticky and cloying, and Marc felt as if he was choking as he leaned against his car. No way could he walk back inside that house and give Laurie the reassurance he knew she needed.

He knew he was behaving badly. He was being a total and utter jerk. Dean had abandoned Laurie practically from the moment she'd told him she was pregnant with Izzy—and here he was, doing exactly the same thing.

Not that Marc intended to abandon Laurie. He'd do the right thing by her. Of *course* he would.

But he really needed to get his head round the situation and be able to think straight before he could talk to her.

And, to get his head round it, it meant he finally had to come to terms with the past.

He reached for his mobile phone. *I'm sorry.*

And then he stopped tapping in the text message. What could he possibly say? He couldn't make this all right. He couldn't walk in and tell her that everything was going to be fine, because right now he was a wreck and he couldn't think straight. He'd say completely the wrong thing and make the situation even worse. He knew he needed to reassure her, but the words wouldn't come. His brain felt sealed up with panic.

Thank God that it was Friday night and he didn't have to struggle through work tomorrow. If it took him the whole night, sitting up and thinking, he'd find the right words. And then he'd talk to her.

He climbed into his car. But instead of driving back to the cottage, he found himself going to the garage to fill his car up with petrol. And then he headed for the place he knew he really needed to go to sort his head out.

London.

He knew he could ring his parents and ask for

a bed for the night, but it was going to be late by the time he got to London and it would be unfair to disturb them. Plus, if he was honest with himself, he didn't really want to talk to anyone about the situation with Laurie. He just needed to be alone with his thoughts.

He pulled into the next lay-by, rang one of the roadside hotel chains and booked a room over the phone with his credit card.

Laurie couldn't sleep. Every time she closed her eyes, she saw the shock on Marc's face as she'd told him about the baby, followed by the distress and the way he'd almost gagged.

I need some air.

Except he hadn't come back. And his mobile phone was switched off. He'd made it very, very clear that he didn't want to know.

What was she going to do? How was she going to explain to Izzy that Marc was out of their lives now? She'd just made the mistake she'd always promised she'd never make, and now her daughter was going to pay for it. Laurie knew that the little girl adored Marc, and she'd be devastated about not seeing him again.

What a mess. Worse still, it wasn't fixable. And somehow she was going to have to find the words to explain to her daughter that Izzy was going to be a big sister, but the baby's daddy wasn't going to be there for any of them.

She curled into a ball, her hands cradled round her stomach. 'I'm not very good at picking daddies,' she said softly to the tiny life inside her. 'But I promise you I'm going to be the best mum in the world to you, and Izzy's going to be the best sister ever. You're not going to miss out on any of the love or any of the things your father can't give you. Because we'll be there.'

If only Marc could've been there for her...

Marc barely slept. Every time he closed his eyes, he saw the accident again. Or the misery on Laurie's face as she told him the news. And no matter how many times he turned over in bed, or pummelled his pillow, he couldn't get comfortable. He couldn't find the words he needed either.

Early the next morning, he went to the open-air market near his old house, knowing that it would be another hour or so before the shops opened and not wanting to wait that long.

To his relief, the florist on the market stall was able to make him a hand-tied arrangement with its own water supply. And when he walked into the churchyard and saw the fresh flowers in the vase on Ginny's grave—proof that her parents had visited very recently—he was glad he'd thought of something that didn't need a vase. He didn't want to displace anything of theirs; he just wanted to give his late wife something of his own.

He placed the flowers on the grave, and sat down cross-legged next to them. 'Freesias, irises and delphiniums. They were always your favourites,' he said softly. And then it was as if a dam had broken and the words spilled out. 'I know I haven't visited you for a while, but I needed to move away, to make a fresh start where I didn't start every day in a black hole thinking that you were just in another room in the house and you'd walk through our bedroom door any second—and when you didn't it was like losing you all over again. And I haven't stopped thinking about you, even though I'm more than a hundred miles away from London.' He paused. 'Gin, I could really do with some of your common sense. I've been given a second chance of happiness, and I've really messed it up.'

He sighed. 'I've met someone. It doesn't mean I'm going to forget you—you're always going to be part of me—but if I were you and you were me, I wouldn't want you to be on your own. I'd want you to meet someone who'd make you happy again and love you as much as I do. And I know that's how it is for you, too.' He stared at the headstone. 'I wanted to make a family with you so much. I should never have left it so late. And I'm sorry I didn't look after you better.'

The brightness of the early morning had given way to clouds. Well, he didn't care if it rained and he got wet. He needed to talk to Ginny. Sort this out in his head.

'You'd like Laurie,' he said. 'In another life, you would've been friends and you'd probably have taught her little girl. Maybe our little girl or boy would've been best friends with Izzy. But that life never happened. We didn't have that chance. And I never thought I'd find love again.'

And then it hit him.

That was exactly what he'd found.

Love.

He really did love Laurie.

He'd fallen in love with her sweetness, her kindness, the dimple in her cheek when she smiled. And she made him feel as if the world was a different place. A better place.

It shocked him to the core. All these weeks he'd been telling himself that they were just having a good time together, that his heart wasn't involved and his barriers were still in place.

Wrong, wrong, wrong. Without him even noticing, they'd melted away, as softly as early-morning mist when the sun came out.

He wasn't sure if it made him feel more exhilarated or terrified. He loved Laurie. They could be happy together. A future full of warmth and laughter and having someone to share the tough bits. It could be wonderful.

And it could all disappear in a second.

Was love worth the risk?

But it was too late to put his barriers up again now. She was in his heart. Along with Izzy. And he knew with rushing certainty that he wanted to be a family with them, and their new baby, and Cocoa.

Or had he just lost that chance?

He raked a hand through his hair. 'I don't know how it happened. *When* it happened. We were just friends. And then…suddenly she was more than that. She's not a replacement for you. She's—well, she's just herself. She has her own place in my life.' He blew out a breath. 'Except I've really messed it up. And I'm not sure if it's fixable.'

He could almost hear Ginny's soft voice telling him to go on.

'It's not tactful telling you this in the circumstances—but you're the one who needs to know,' he said. 'Laurie's going to have a baby. My baby. We didn't plan it. And I've been so selfish and left her waiting, because I don't know what to say and I can't quite get my head around it.'

Why? What was stopping him? The questions echoed in his head as clearly as if she was actually talking to him.

He had to be honest with himself, too. 'It scares me stupid that I could lose her and our baby, the way I lost you, and bits of me think maybe I shouldn't take the risk.' He sighed. 'And bits of me... I want to make a family with her, Gin. I want Izzy to call me "Dad". I want to take the chance of happiness with both hands and hold it close.' He paused. 'I know I didn't take care of you the way I should've done. This is like a second chance for me. Is it so bad of me to want to take it?'

Silence. Well, of course. How would he get an answer?

'I love her, Gin. It's not the same as it was with you. I'm older, we haven't known each other for so long, and there's still a lot about her that surprises me. But I know I'll be happy with her. And I know that you'd love her too. I want to spend the rest of my life with her. *If* she'll have me.'

The sun came out and shone straight into his eyes. It was almost, he thought, as if Ginny was giving him her blessing.

'Thank you,' he said quietly. 'I might not come and see you here that often, but you're not just here in the churchyard. You're here, too. Always.' He placed his hand over his heart. 'And I'll grow delphiniums for you in my garden and think of you when they bloom.' He stood up, pressed his fingers to his mouth and then to her headstone. 'God bless.'

Back at his car, Marc called Laurie. When her landline went through to the answering-machine, he hung up. This wasn't something he could say in a message. He needed to say it to her.

Was she out, or was she call-screening? He wouldn't blame her if it was the latter. But he tried her mobile anyway.

For a moment, he thought it was going to go through to voicemail. But then she answered. 'Hello?'

She sounded terrible, her voice cracked and strained by lack of sleep. Which was all his fault.

'Laurie, it's Marc.' Stupid. She'd already know that from his name flashing up on the screen of her phone.

'Where are you?' she asked.

'In London.' Honesty compelled him to add, 'I've just been to Ginny's grave.'

'Oh.'

'We need to talk.'

'Right now,' she said, 'I'm not too sure if I want to talk to you.'

'I don't blame you. I've been a complete idiot, and I'm so sorry. But I'm not Dean. I know I walked out on you last night, and I shouldn't have done that. I panicked. I'm completely in the wrong. And I want to apologise to you properly.'

She said nothing, but he heard a tiny sob, quickly muffled.

'Laurie, I'm sorry. I reacted badly. I don't have an excuse, but I needed to get my head around— well, several things. I'm driving home now. And I know I deserve absolutely nothing from you, but right now I really want to hold you. To make things right between us. Can I come and see you?'

She gulped. 'Yes.'

Should he tell her how he felt about her right now? Or should he wait so she could see his face and know he meant it?

He decided to wait. 'I'll see you soon. And everything's going to be all right, Laurie. I promise.'

'Don't make promises you can't keep.'

'This one I can definitely keep,' he said softly.

'Drive safely. Don't—don't take any risks.'

'I won't. Take risks, I mean. I'll be home as soon as I can.'

The traffic was terrible, but eventually he made it back to Norfolk and parked outside Laurie's house.

'Where's Izzy?' he asked when she opened the door.

'With my parents. I didn't want her overhearing any of this.'

'You look terrible.' Her eyes were red and swollen, and she'd obviously spent much of the night crying.

She lifted her chin. 'I told Izzy—and my parents—that I had a cold.'

Guilt flooded through him. She was pregnant, and he should've taken care of her, not left her to get on with it and be miserable.

'I'm so sorry.' He touched her cheek with the backs of his fingers. 'Do you want me to get you a cold flannel for your eyes?'

'No.' Her mouth thinned. 'You said we needed to talk.'

He exhaled sharply. 'We do.'

'You'd better come in.' She stepped to the side, and her body language was screaming, Don't touch. And even Cocoa was looking at him reproachfully, rather than wagging his tail and insisting on having his tummy rubbed.

Marc knew it was what he deserved. He followed her into the kitchen; when she sat down, he did the same.

'Firstly, I'm sorry about last night. I panicked.'

'I noticed.'

'I'm not making an excuse. What I did was unfair to you. And I'm scared I'm going to say the wrong thing now and hurt you. I don't mean to.'

'You don't want to know about the baby. You've already made that clear.'

'No. That's not it at all.' He blew out a breath. 'I owe you total honesty, Laurie. Some of it might be painful. But I guess this is a warts-and-all conversation. Will you hear me out?'

She was silent for so long that he thought she was going to tell him to leave.

And then she nodded.

'I've been here before, Lauric. The thrill of knowing that I'm going to be a dad, all the plans and the love and the joy. And then the black hole when I lost Ginny and the baby. And last night… It just brought everything back. The crash. How I felt. The yawning emptiness. I panicked. That's why I walked out. Not because I don't want you or the baby or Izzy—I do, I want *all* of you—but because that potential of loss scares me stupid.'

'There's always a risk of losing something. But if you stand on the sidelines and you never take that risk, then you've lost it all anyway,' she pointed out.

'Yes. You're right. Last night, I should've pushed all of that out of my head. And what I should've told you—'

'No.' She shook her head. 'Don't say anything you don't mean. I've been here before.'

'No, you haven't. Not with me. Laurie…I love you.'

She stared at him, looking shocked. 'You love me?'

'I have done for ages. Probably since I first met you, but I've been in denial about a lot of things so I can't be sure of that. But I've definitely loved you all summer. Maybe since Izzy and I made that ice-cream sundae together.'

Her eyes were suspiciously shiny, and he knew she was close to crying. 'Oh, Marc. I love you, too. Except…I'm scared,' she whispered.

'I know. But I'm not Dean. I know I left last night, because I was overwhelmed and I was selfish and put my needs before yours. But I want to make that right now. And I can assure you that I'm not planning to dump you. Or to go off with any of our patients.'

'I know you wouldn't be unfaithful. You're not the type.' She lifted her chin. 'But are you going to walk out on me every time it gets tough? Because if you are, I'm better off without you. I'm not putting Izzy on a rollercoaster like that. Or the baby. Or me.'

He deserved that, he knew. 'No, I'm not. I can't prove it to you, but last night was different. This morning I got my head together, I'm ready to move on from the past. It still scares me stupid that I could lose you and the baby, but you're right—it's worth the risk.'

'Are you sure?'

'I'm sure. And it doesn't matter that we didn't plan to have this baby,' Marc said. 'I want to be a family with you and Izzy and her little brother or sister. And it's not to replace Ginny or the baby I never got to meet, before you start thinking that. This is *our* baby. And I want the three of you—and Cocoa—more than you'll ever know.'

This time the tears spilled down her cheeks. 'Oh, Marc.'

He went round to her side of the table, scooped her up and settled her on his lap. 'We need to go public now,' he said. 'I want the world to know I'm your partner. And I want to be Izzy's dad.'

Her eyes brightened with hope. 'Really?'

'Really. It isn't about being a biological parent, it's all about being there—and I'm going to be there for all of you. You, Izzy, our baby, Cocoa. I'm going to be there.'

'Oh, Marc.' She rested her head on his shoulder and wept.

He held her close. 'Don't cry, honey.'

'It must be hormones.' Her voice was shaky. 'I'm never this wet.'

'I know. You've had to be strong and independent for so long—but now you can share the worries with me.' He stroked her hair. 'I should be doing this in a fancy restaurant or under the stars or when the sun's setting over the sea—but I don't want to wait to ask you. If Izzy gives me her permission, will you marry me?'

She cried even harder, and Marc panicked.

'What's wrong? Don't you want to marry me?'

'Yes, I do—of course I do—but you're going to ask Izzy.' She dragged in a breath. 'You care about her feelings.'

'Of course I do. It's a big thing for her. She's had you all to herself for her entire life, and having to share you might be hard for her. I want to reassure her that she's not sharing you, she's getting me as well. And if Izzy wants me to be her dad, I'd be hugely, hugely proud.' He kissed her gently. 'And then I guess I need to ask your dad's permission.'

Laurie's smile was slightly wobbly, but it made him feel as if the sun had come out. 'I have a feeling you'll get it.'

The next day, Marc took Izzy to feed the ducks.

'You're my friend, right?' he asked.

She nodded, beaming. 'You're one of my best friends.'

Now for the big question. 'How would you like to be my daughter as well as my friend?'

She looked thoughtful, and was silent for a long, long time, just throwing bread to the ducks. 'No,' she said eventually.

Marc felt sick. He'd thought that he got on well with the little girl; but if he didn't have Izzy's blessing there was no way he could marry Laurie. It just wouldn't work. 'Why not?' he asked, careful to keep his voice neutral.

'It's not because I don't like you,' she said, 'but I don't want to leave Mummy and live with you. She'd be lonely without me, even though she has Cocoa.'

Marc nearly dropped to his knees in relief. He smiled. 'You don't have to leave your mum, Izzy. What I mean is that I'd like to marry your mum and make you my daughter, so you'd be Izzy Bailey rather than Izzy Grant. Your mum would be Dr Bailey, like me. And we'd all live together with Cocoa.'

'So you'd be my real daddy?' she asked.

'If you want me to be, yes.'

'And I could—' Her eyes widened. 'I could call you Daddy?'

He wrapped her in a hug. 'I'd love that. I'd be so proud to be your dad, Iz.'

She hugged him back. 'Does that mean I'll have a little brother or sister? Matthew in my class, his mum got married last year and now he's got a baby sister.'

'I'll see what I can do,' Marc said. He and Laurie had agreed to wait a little while before telling Izzy about the baby, but he could reassure Laurie now that that particular worry was out of the way. 'Shall we go and tell your mum the good news?'

'You bet!'

Laurie's family, predictably, was delighted to hear the news. So was Marc's. As the news spread in the village, Laurie was overwhelmed with good wishes from everyone.

But there were still shadows in Marc's eyes, and she had a pretty good idea why.

'I think,' she said softly, 'we need to call in a favour from my parents and get them to look after Iz for the weekend.'

'Why?'

'Because you need to make your peace with

Ginny's parents.' She took a deep breath. 'And there's something I need to do. A promise I need to make. To Ginny.'

Marc held her close. 'You're amazing. Do you know that?'

'Keep telling me. I'm happy to hear it.' She kissed him. 'You're amazing, too. And this is going to work out just fine.'

CHAPTER THIRTEEN

THE following weekend, Marc and Laurie visited Ginny's grave together.

She knelt down by the grave. 'In another life, we would've been friends and our children would've played together,' she said softly. 'Marc's always going to love you. I promise I'll never take that away from you, but love isn't a fixed thing. It expands and grows, so he has room in his heart for me and Izzy, too. And our baby. And if it's a girl, maybe you won't mind if we name her after you. If I were in your shoes, I'd like to think that that's how he'd remember me.' She dragged in a breath. 'I just want you to know that I'll look after him. That I'll do my best to make him happy. And that we'll make the most of having a second chance.'

She left Marc to make his own peace with Ginny, waiting for him on the bench outside the churchyard. Finally, he came to join her, and his eyes were slightly red.

'Are you OK?' she asked.

'No.' His voice sounded choked.

She hugged him. 'Sorry. I know that was hard for you.'

'It isn't that.' He held her close. 'Laurie Grant, you're an incredible woman and I really, really love you. My world's changed so much since you've been in it.'

'I love you, too,' she said softly.

'Come on. I'll take you to my parents, and then I'll go and see the Frasers.'

'Are you sure you don't want me to come with you?'

He nodded. 'Maybe they'll agree to meet you once I've talked to them. But this is something I have to face on my own.'

'Even if they won't talk to you, Marc, remember that love stretches. You're not doing anything wrong, and you're not pushing Ginny out of your life.'

'I know.' He held her for a moment longer. 'Let's go.'

* * *

Walking up the path to Ginny's parents' house brought back a flood of bad memories for Marc. Of the way they'd screamed at him. The way they'd refused to forgive him.

Two years ago.

Time was meant to be a healer. But would time have changed Carol and Stephen Fraser's attitude towards him?

There was only one way to find out.

He took a deep breath, and rang the doorbell.

Carol Fraser opened the door and stared at him in seeming disbelief. 'What are *you* doing here?' Her lip curled with bitterness.

'I need to talk to you,' Marc said quietly.

She shook her head. 'I don't want to talk to you.'

'I don't blame you for hating me,' he said. 'Believe me, I've hated myself.'

Stephen joined her at the door, clearly having overheard the conversation. 'Our daughter's dead.'

'And nothing I can do can bring her back. I wish I could. I wish things could've been different.'

'I wish you'd been driving and it had been you,' Stephen said, his face suffused with colour.

'For a long time, so did I,' Marc said. 'I need to talk to you both. Please may I come in?'

They just stood there in silence, giving him a bitter stare, and Marc thought that they were going to refuse. But finally Carol nodded. Saying nothing, she and Stephen stepped aside and let him.

Marc followed them into the living room and waited for them to ask him to sit down. When they didn't, he remained standing.

'It's been more than two years now,' he said. 'I'll always love Ginny, but she wouldn't want me to spend the rest of my life on my own.'

'You're asking our permission to see someone?' Stephen asked, his tone full of disbelief.

'No. But I'd rather you heard this from me than from someone else. I've met someone. We're going to get married.'

Carol's eyes narrowed. 'Why are you telling us?'

'Because,' he said, 'I've learned something. Love stretches. It's not a thing that you ladle out into bowls for a while and then the pan's empty. Ginny loved you very much. Before she was killed—'

'Murdered,' Stephen cut in.

'Killed,' Marc repeated gently. 'It was an accident—and it's taken me two years to come to terms with that. Yes, I should've been driving. But there are so many variables. If we'd left earlier or later, if we'd taken a different route, if the other driver had paid attention to the road instead of to his mobile phone—but they're all ifs. And they didn't happen. We've lost Ginny, and we have to come to terms with that.'

'I'll *never* come to terms with that. Do you have any idea what it's like to lose your only child?' Carol demanded.

'Actually,' he said, 'I do. And every day I think how old our little one would be, and wonder what he or she would be doing now. I've avoided children for two years because I couldn't handle it—and that's the baby I never got to meet. But you had thirty years of loving Ginny. Thirty years of memories. And maybe it's time to hang onto the good stuff and let the bad go.'

'How do you think we'll ever get over it?' Stephen asked.

'I don't know. But—look, before the accident, we all got on well. You know I loved your daughter, and I would've done anything for her.'

'But you didn't, did you?' Stephen's lip curled. 'You didn't look after her enough.'

'I made one wrong choice. And I have to live with that every day of my life,' Marc said softly. 'But I've learned from what happened. And I'm asking you for a second chance. If I'd been the one who'd died in the crash, I'd like to think that Ginny would've moved on with her life, found someone who loved her as much as I did and would make her happy. And I'd like to think that she would've stayed in touch with my parents, too, still looked on them as part of her extended family.'

There was a long, long silence and Marc thought maybe he'd gone too far.

'That's what you're asking from us?' Carol asked.

'Yes.'

'Ginny was all we had,' Stephen said.

'I know. But, when I married her, you had me

as well.' He paused. 'You still have me. If you want that.'

'How can we bear to see you with someone else in our daughter's place?' Carol asked.

'That isn't how it is. Laurie isn't in Ginny's place. She's not pushing Ginny out of my life. I'll still have Ginny's photo up with all the others, and...' He blew out a breath. 'Well, hey, I can't make things any worse than they are, so I might as well tell you the rest. We're going to have a baby. It wasn't planned, but we're thrilled about it. And so is Laurie's little girl. If we have a daughter, we'd like to call her Ginny—so your daughter's memory is still going to live on with us.'

'Call *your* child after *our* daughter,' Stephen echoed, shaking his head.

'In another life,' Marc said, 'if Ginny and I had moved to Norfolk, I think she and Laurie would've been friends. I would've known Laurie through work and Ginny would've known her through school. And you would probably have met her at our house and liked her.'

'And yet you're putting her in our daughter's place,' Stephen said.

'Not in Ginny's place. In her *own* place in my life,' Marc said gently. 'Laurie doesn't look anything like Ginny, but she has that same warmth, that same caring spirit. She's a doctor—that's how I met her. At work. She's taught me that love stretches, that even when life is rough you can still make the best of what you have. And I hope that you'll find it in you to do that with us. It's not going to be the same—of *course* it's not—but this way you still get to have that extended family.'

'And she's OK with this?' Stephen asked.

Marc nodded. 'We've talked it over. She came with me to Ginny's grave this morning. To tell Ginny that she'd look after me and make sure her memory lives on.'

Carol looked thoughtful. 'Where is this Laurie now?'

'With my parents. I didn't think it would be fair to bring her to meet you without talking to you first. Just so you know, my parents like her very much. They've welcomed her into the family.' He paused. 'It's your decision now. If you'd like to meet her, we'd both be delighted about it. And if you meet her it might reassure you that Ginny's not going to be packed away and forgotten about.'

They said nothing.

'I'll give you some time to think about it. We're going to be in London until about four today. If you'd like us to meet you somewhere today, just call me and tell me where and we'll be there. Otherwise I'll leave it to you until you feel ready.' He swallowed hard. 'I'll go now. And I'm sorry. I should've tried harder to talk to you, a long time before now. I should've looked after you better, the way Ginny would've done with my parents.' Even though the Frasers had made it very clear they hadn't wanted anything to do with him and would always blame him for Ginny's death, Marc knew he could and should have tried harder, for her sake. 'I'll see myself out. But I hope from now on that we can maybe come to some kind of understanding. Some kind of peace. For Ginny's sake.'

They still said nothing.

And he had nothing left to say right at that moment. Though he would try again, he thought as he left. Maybe next time he'd try a different tack.

He was almost back at his parents' house when his phone beeped to signal a text message. He let it wait until he'd parked the car, then fished his phone out of his pocket. He'd half expected the text to be from Laurie—but it was from Carol, saying she'd like to meet Laurie.

Thank you. What time and where? he texted back.

It was a while before she replied, and he was just getting out of his car when his phone beeped again. *The park opposite our house, two o'clock.*

It would be tight, but it was doable.

Laurie and his parents met him with a hug. 'How did it go?'

'It was fairly awkward,' he admitted. 'They still blame me—and they were pretty shocked when I told them about you and the baby.'

'It can't have been easy for you either,' Laurie said.

'It wasn't.' He paused. 'But they've had time to think about it, and they've just texted me. They want to meet you.'

By the time two o'clock came, Laurie was incredibly nervous. This would be Marc's second chance from his in-laws. What if they decided they didn't like her, and changed their minds?

As if Marc could guess what she was thinking, he squeezed her hand. 'Don't worry. This will be fine. Just be yourself.'

She gave him a wry smile. 'Hey, well, this was my idea. I can't chicken out now.'

But as they drew nearer to the couple sitting on the park bench, she felt sick. Please, please, let them like her. Let them give Marc the second chance he deserved.

Marc introduced them swiftly.

'Thank you for agreeing to meet me.' Laurie said. 'I didn't know Ginny, but Marc talks about her, and in her photographs she looks like a really lovely woman. I know this must be really hard for you, seeing me with Marc. And you had such a terrible loss, your only child—I can't even begin to imagine what it would be like to lose my little girl.' Even the thought of it made her blood freeze. 'I think I'd be beside myself.'

Carol swallowed. 'Marc said you had a little girl.'

'Izzy. She's five.' Laurie took her phone out

of her handbag and showed Carol one of the photographs.

'She looks very sweet.' Carol looked misty-eyed. 'I remember Ginny at that age. She used to chatter away all the time.'

'So does Izzy. And she loves decorating cup-cakes—you wouldn't believe how many different coloured sprinkles she uses.'

'Ginny loved doing that, too.' Unchecked, a tear trickled down Carol's face.

Laurie hated to see her distress. Unable to hold back any longer, she hugged Carol. 'I'm not your daughter, Mrs Fraser. I can never even begin to take her place, and I wouldn't ever be so insensitive as to try, but you're still part of Marc's family. And I hope that maybe one day you'll be able to consider yourself part of mine, too.'

Carol was shaking. 'Marc says you're having a baby.'

Laurie nodded. 'And if she's a girl, we'd really like her to share your daughter's name—so Ginny's memory is still going to live on with us.'

Carol broke down completely, holding Laurie as tightly as Laurie was holding her. 'Marc was right—you do remind me of my Ginny. You look nothing like her but you've got that same caring way about you.' She dragged in a breath. 'Ginny was a teacher.'

'I'm a doctor, so I guess it's a similar thing—we look after people.'

Carol pulled away so she could look Laurie in the eye. 'And you're not going to push Ginny out of Marc's life?'

'Of course I'm not. She'll always be there in his heart, and she'll always have a picture up in our house. And you'll always be welcome there, too.' Laurie felt the tears spill over her own eyelashes.

Awkwardly, Marc patted her shoulder and Stephen rested his hand over Carol's.

Carol turned to Marc. 'You're right. The accident wasn't your fault. Yes, you should've been driving, that night, but you weren't the one on the wrong side of the road.' She swallowed hard. 'I blamed you because it was easier having someone to be angry with—something to fill the hole Ginny left behind.'

'Better to fill that hole with love than with anger,' Laurie said. 'Love and hope. Because there's always something good to find about the world.'

Stephen stared at her. 'That's—that's the sort of thing Ginny would've said. She…she would have liked you.' He looked at Marc. 'That second chance you talked about? I think we all need that. Carol and I haven't been fair to you. And you lost her, too.' He held his hand out for Marc to shake. 'Maybe we should focus on the good memories, like you said. Celebrate her instead of missing what we never had a chance to share. And I hope—' His breath hitched 'I hope you two will be happy together.'

'Thank you,' Marc said, and shook his hand.

CHAPTER FOURTEEN

LIFE, Laurie thought, didn't get any better than this. Preparations for the wedding were in full swing; the church was booked, the reception was going to be at the local hotel, and Tina's mum was making the wedding cake. Yvonne, Fiona, Izzy, Georgia and Molly were brides-maids; Joe was the best man; and she knew that Marc was relieved that the Frasers had actually accepted their invitation to the wedding. Laurie and Izzy had rented out their house and moved in with Marc, and Marc had had the news that morning that the landlord was happy to sell them the house.

It was all working out perfectly.

Laurie was on her way to some house calls at the care home at the outskirts of town, singing along to the radio, when a cat ran out in front of her. Not wanting to hit the animal, she braked hard—but then she felt a jolt, heard a bang, and the car was careening out of her control and heading toward a wall.

Time seemed to slow down and speed up all at once.

Emergency stop. Right. She needed to put her foot on the clutch and combine it with short, sharp pumps on the brake so it didn't lock up. Praying as she did so, she pumped the brake.

And then the car hit the wall.

The seat belt locked, holding her away from the steering-wheel, and Laurie felt a sharp pain across her abdomen.

Oh, God. *The baby.* She struggled to take some deep, even breaths, aware that she was shaking. The baby needed oxygen. And she had to calm down; stress wasn't good for the baby.

She couldn't feel any wetness between her legs, but that didn't mean anything. If the accident had caused her to have a placental abruption, there wouldn't necessarily be any blood yet. The bleed could be masked by its position, and she would just start to have symptoms of shock as the bleed grew.

She wanted Marc. Right now.

Though, at the same time, how could she ring

him and tell him she'd crashed the car? The last time she'd brought all his nightmares back, the night she'd told him she was pregnant, he'd walked out on her. Would he let her down again?

For the baby's sake, she hoped not.

And she wasn't sure what scared her most. Marc's reaction or her situation.

She had to sort this out. Right now. And, please, please, let her really be able to rely on Marc.

She was shaking even harder as she pushed the switch on her hazard lights and tried to release her seat belt. It took her several goes before she managed it; then she reached down into the passenger footwell to grab her handbag. She misdialled Marc's number twice, but finally his phone started to ring.

'Marc?'

'No, it's Phyllis. He's switched his mobile through to the surgery reception.'

Of course he had. He'd be with a patient. Laurie couldn't think straight. She took a deep breath. 'Phyllis, I need to speak to him. I wouldn't ask if it wasn't urgent. Please.'

'Are you all right, love?'

Yes. No. She didn't have a clue. All she knew was that she wanted Marc. 'I need Marc.'

'All right, love. Hang on in there.'

Marc's phone beeped, and he frowned. Phyllis would know from the practice computer system that he was with a patient and shouldn't be interrupted. So she'd only be calling him if it was something important.

'I'm sorry, would you mind if I take that?' he asked his patient.

'Sure, go ahead.'

'Marc, I've got Laurie for you,' Phyllis said.

His frown deepened. Laurie worked here herself, so she'd never normally interrupt him when he was with a patient. He knew she was out doing some house calls; but if she wanted a second opinion on a patient's condition, she'd leave a message for Phyllis to grab him between patients, and wait for him to call her back. What was going on?

He suddenly had a nasty feeling something was seriously wrong.

'Laurie? Are you all right?'

'I— Marc, I'm all right, at least I think I

am, but I had an accident.' Her voice sounded wobbly.

He thought of Ginny and felt sick. No. This couldn't happen all over again. It just *couldn't*. He struggled to sound calm. 'What happened?'

'I had to brake hard and I think I must've hit a pothole. I slid over the road, and I think my tyre blew.' She was sounding more and more scared. 'The car hit a wall. I don't think I can drive it any more.'

'Where are you?' he asked urgently.

'The other side of town from the surgery. I was on my way out to Whitegates Care Home.'

'I'll come and get you.' He clenched his fists, forcing himself to stay calm. 'Can you smell petrol?'

'I don't think so— Oh, my God, I'm using my mobile phone and the car might be leaking!'

'It's OK. Don't panic. You would've blown up by now if there was a problem.' He hoped he sounded much more cool and casual than he felt, and that injecting a bit of dark medic humour would calm her down. 'OK. Deep breath and put your hazard lights on, honey.'

'Done it already.'

'Good. You're safest to stay in the car, so don't move. I'm leaving now.' He put the phone down and turned to his patient. 'I'm sorry, I would never normally ask you to come back later or to wait to see another doctor, but I really have to go right now—this is an emergency.'

'I was trying not to listen in, but it sounded like you were talking about an accident. Is it Dr Grant?'

'Yes.'

'Oh, dear. I hope she's all right.'

So do I, thought Marc. So do I. 'Thank you. I'll get Phyllis to book you in.' He ushered his patient out of the consulting room then gave Phyllis a quick rundown of the situation.

'You go, love. I'll sort out the patients, and I'll ring Diane to ask her to pick Izzy up from school,' Phyllis said. 'Give Laurie my love, and keep me posted, OK?'

He nodded. 'Thanks. I will.'

He drove out of town in the direction Laurie had taken, and blanched when he saw her car ploughed into the wall. It brought back way too many bad memories of the accident that had taken Ginny from him.

Please, please, don't let Laurie be taken from him, too.

But right now he had to put her feelings before his. She needed him, and he wasn't going to let her down ever again.

He parked behind her, switched on his hazard lights and waited just long enough for the car behind him to overtake them. Seconds later he had Laurie's car door open and his arms wrapped round her.

'Are you OK?' he asked.

'I think so. Shaky. But OK.'

'I'd better check you over.' He took her pulse. 'OK. I'm happy with that. And it's probably better than mine is right now.' Her blood pressure, too, was normal. That was a good sign. And she wasn't showing any symptoms of hypovolaemic shock. 'Did you black out or anything?'

'No, and I didn't hit my head. I'll probably have a bruise from the seat belt, though,' she said ruefully. 'I called the police to tell them I had an accident but nobody else was involved, and I called the insurance company. They're sending a pick-up truck out to fetch the car. They won't be long.'

'I'll drive you home,' Marc said. 'Call them on the way and tell them I'm taking you home and then I'll be back. You need to rest—and I think you ought to have tomorrow off. Actually, I might call in the big guns and get Diane to babysit you.'

She shook her head. 'There's no need. I was pretty scared when it happened, but it was just the shock and the speed of it. I'm fine now. Marc, you're overreacting.'

'No, I'm not,' he said firmly. 'I'm not going to risk anything happening to you, Laurie. Don't argue.'

Laurie knew why he was worrying. Because of the last accident he'd had to deal with. But he was here. And he'd put her needs first without a moment's hesitation.

She wrapped her arms round him. 'You really don't have to worry. But I get why you are.'

'Yeah. And you'll rest?'

'I'll rest,' she promised.

And although she thought he was definitely overreacting, she agreed to take the next day off work.

* * *

She was pottering around the garden when it struck her that something was odd. Something was missing.

When she worked out what it was, she went cold. *She hadn't felt the baby move for quite a while.* She knew that the baby was well insulated, but supposing the accident had done more damage than she'd thought?

No.

It was unthinkable.

She drummed her fingers on her belly, hoping to persuade the baby into kicking back.

No response.

She sat with her hands pressed again her stomach, praying for the baby to kick hard enough for her to feel it.

Still nothing.

Maybe she was panicking over nothing. She had a definite bruise from the seat belt, so maybe that was the problem. Maybe her body could only concentrate on one feeling at a time. Besides, she'd only just started to feel the baby's movements—earlier than she had with Izzy.

But her worries grew all morning.

Marc rang her during his break. 'Everything OK?'

'I...' Laurie dragged in a breath and tried to keep the sobs back, but she failed.

'Laurie? Laurie, what's wrong? Talk to me, honey, tell me,' he demanded.

'Marc, I can't feel the baby move, and I'm— I'm—I'm so *scared!*' she burst out.

'I'm on my way.'

He was with her in five minutes, and she knew he'd broken every speed limit on the way. He'd brought the hand-held Doppler ultrasound machine from the surgery with him. He pressed the transducer to her stomach and they both listened to the built-in speaker, but there was none of the clop-clop-clop they were both desperate to hear, the rapid beat of the baby's heart.

'Don't panic,' he said. 'This thing looks as if it came in with the ark and it's probably too old to be working properly. Or I've put it in the wrong place.'

He tried again.

Still nothing.

He'd already lost one baby, with Ginny. And now they couldn't hear the baby's heartbeat—so the chances were high that he was going to lose another. Laurie didn't think she could bear it.

He held her tightly and kissed her. 'I'm going to call the hospital, OK? Try not to worry.'

After a quick conversation he put the phone down. 'I've spoken to one of the midwives in the maternity unit and they're going to give you a scan at the hospital. Come on, I'm driving.' He gave her a hug. 'It's going to be fine. It's probably because you're worried, and maybe a bit bruised, so you're not feeling things the way you should be. And it's still early to be feeling the baby kick, in any case.' He tried to convince himself.

'You feel it earlier with the second one,' she reminded him.

'And the surgery definitely needs a more up-to-date Doppler. It's a machine error, OK?'

She knew he was trying to reassure her, but it wasn't working. She swallowed hard. 'I can't bear the idea of losing our baby,' she whispered.

'You're not losing our baby.'

'If I hadn't had that accident...'

'That's my line,' he said, and kissed her.

'Come on. Breathe. I'm here, and everything's going to be just fine.'

Laurie was really relieved to be able to lean on Marc, even more so than when she'd called him from the car accident. She'd worried that he might crumble and leave her to deal with it, unable to face a similar situation to the one that had wrecked his life before. But he was just brilliant—calm, reassuring and completely in charge. There wasn't even a hint of panic in his eyes. He was there for her. For the baby.

She was numb throughout the drive to hospital and couldn't concentrate on a thing. Marc parked the car, then held her hand all the way as they walked to the maternity unit.

Her name was written on a whiteboard, under the word 'Emergency'. Laurie went cold at the sight.

He kept his hand tightly wrapped round hers. 'You know as well as I do what that means. It's "Emergency" because it isn't a scan that's been booked in as routine by the midwives. *Breathe*,' he said, making her take deep breaths in and out. He fetched her a plastic cup of water and made her sit down in the waiting room. 'Sip this slowly,' he said. 'I'm going to let the receptionist know that we're here.'

It could only have been a few minutes but it felt as if a lifetime had gone by when one of the obstetricians came in and introduced himself.

Marc filled him in on the details. 'Laurie's sixteen weeks pregnant. It's her second baby. She had a minor car accident yesterday; she didn't think she was hurt, but she can't feel the baby move today. I used the surgery's Doppler to hear the heartbeat but I couldn't get a result—I think the machine was playing up, but obviously we need a bit of reassurance.'

'OK. Try not to worry.' The obstetrician smiled at them. 'We'll do our best to see what's going on. Come through with me, and we'll get the portable scanner going.'

Laurie lay on the bed as the doctor directed, lifting her top up. He placed conductive gel on her stomach. In theory, this was just like the twelve-week scan she'd had the previous month, when she and Marc had been thrilled to see their baby on the screen—but this felt much, much scarier.

Laurie couldn't see the screen and she knew that Marc couldn't either.

Panic seeped through her. Was the doctor keeping the screen turned away from them because it was bad news and he was trying to work out how to break it?

Her hand tightened round Marc's. This was unbearable.

The doctor was frowning and moving the transceiver on her stomach, and the seeping panic turned into a flood. Please, please, *please*, don't let them lose their baby. Please, don't let Marc have to go through this again.

But then the doctor smiled at them both and turned the screen round so they could see it.

'I'm pleased to say that here we have one baby. Kicking very happily, even though you can't feel it. So there's absolutely nothing to worry about.'

Laurie felt her face crumple, and then she sobbed with relief.

Marc was shaking, and when she looked at him she could see that his eyes were wet, too.

'You can see the heart beating, here. It's very strong, and there's absolutely nothing to worry about,' the doctor said again. 'What I'd recommend is that you go home now and try to get some rest.'

'You bet she will,' Marc said. 'I'm going to wrap her in cotton wool.'

Laurie felt her eyes widen. 'Marc, you can't do that.'

'No? Fine,' he said. 'I'll call your mum. And mine. And if they don't make you rest, I'll call in Fiona, Tina, Phyllis—and, actually, yes, I think Carol as well. And she'll be really strict with you. You don't stand a chance.'

Laurie knew when she was beaten. And she was so, so grateful that he was taking care of her like this. 'OK, I get the picture. I'll behave. I'll rest.'

'Good, because I'm not risking anything with you.' He held her close. 'I love you, Laurie Grant. And I want you right as rain on our wedding day. So, to my way of thinking, that means you have four weeks of rest, starting from this very second—and I'll run any errand you ask of me.'

'Even if it's fetching me chocolate ice cream from the twenty-four-hour supermarket at two in the morning because I have a craving?' she tested.

'Yes.'

'Or running the bridesmaids over for a dress fitting?'

'Yes.'

'Checking the flowers?'

'Anything you like, as long as you rest,' he said, and kissed her.

Four weeks later, it was the sunniest November morning Laurie could ever remember. The day when she was going to become Dr Bailey.

She and Izzy had stayed overnight at her parents' house, because Marc had gone superstitious and insisted on observing all the traditions. The senior bridesmaids were all ready, and the three junior bridesmaids were all thrilled to be allowed to wear nail polish as well as have flowers in their hair.

'Ready, love?' Roderick asked.

'I'm ready.'

Diane arranged her veil in place. 'You look lovely, darling.'

'Mummy, you look like a princess,' Izzy sighed happily. 'And Daddy's going to be a prince.'

'Definitely my prince charming,' Laurie said with a grin. Even if he was forever nagging her to sit down and put her feet up, and she knew he'd make her pace herself in the dancing.

And she loved every second of her wedding day. Driving in the old-fashioned car with her father to the church; walking up the aisle on her father's arm towards Marc; the first kiss with her new husband; the hugs and warm congratulations of all their guests, including Dean's parents and Ginny's.

But Izzy stole the show when she gave her speech. 'Uncle Joe and Granddad have already said welcome to the family,' she said, 'but I want to say it too. Because Marc's really special and he makes my mummy smile. He's my daddy now they're married, so I don't have to call him Marc any more.' She ran over to him and hugged him. He lifted her up, resting her against his hip. 'I love you, Daddy,' she said, and Laurie had to blink back the tears.

'I love you too, Izzy Bailey.' His voice was slightly croaky with emotion. 'And I'd like to make a toast to the women in my new family. Laurie Bailey, my wife. Izzy Bailey, my daughter. And, according to the doctor at yesterday's scan, we have a third: Ginny Bailey. It's going to be another four months or so before we meet her, but I reckon she's going to be just as gorgeous as her mum and her big sister and I'm going to love her just as much. The Bailey women. Because they're amazing.'

'Amazing,' everyone echoed, lifting their glasses.

EPILOGUE

Twenty-four weeks later

'MY LOVELY, lovely girls.' Marc couldn't remember ever feeling this proud and happy. Sitting on the side of his wife's hospital bed, with their day-old daughter in her arms, and their five-and-a-half-year-old sitting on his knee—he'd declared a long time ago that he didn't care that Izzy wasn't biologically his, because she was *definitely* his—he'd rate this as the best moment of his entire life.

'Ginny's a really pretty name,' Izzy said with satisfaction. 'A princess name. I'm going to read her all my princess stories. And she can wear all my dressing up clothes when she's big enough, because I'll be too big for them then.'

'That,' Marc said, 'sounds absolutely perfect.'

* * * * *

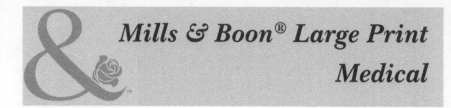

Mills & Boon® Large Print
Medical

September

NYC ANGELS: REDEEMING THE PLAYBOY	Carol Marinelli
NYC ANGELS: HEIRESS'S BABY SCANDAL	Janice Lynn
ST PIRAN'S: THE WEDDING!	Alison Roberts
SYDNEY HARBOUR HOSPITAL: EVIE'S BOMBSHELL	Amy Andrews
THE PRINCE WHO CHARMED HER	Fiona McArthur
HIS HIDDEN AMERICAN BEAUTY	Connie Cox

October

NYC ANGELS: UNMASKING DR SERIOUS	Laura Iding
NYC ANGELS: THE WALLFLOWER'S SECRET	Susan Carlisle
CINDERELLA OF HARLEY STREET	Anne Fraser
YOU, ME AND A FAMILY	Sue MacKay
THEIR MOST FORBIDDEN FLING	Melanie Milburne
THE LAST DOCTOR SHE SHOULD EVER DATE	Louisa George

November

NYC ANGELS: FLIRTING WITH DANGER	Tina Beckett
NYC ANGELS: TEMPTING NURSE SCARLET	Wendy S. Marcus
ONE LIFE CHANGING MOMENT	Lucy Clark
P.S. YOU'RE A DADDY!	Dianne Drake
RETURN OF THE REBEL DOCTOR	Joanna Neil
ONE BABY STEP AT A TIME	Meredith Webber

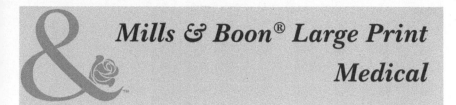

Mills & Boon® Large Print
Medical

December

January

February